A STEEPLECHASE
FOR LOVE

Walking back from the stables the Duke passed the wrong turning to The Hall he had taken on the day of his arrival.

Instinctively he glanced down the path, wondering if he would again see the beautiful girl who had directed him to the front door.

'*Helsa*', he thought to himself.

No woman he had ever known had had that name and it certainly suited her.

He felt disappointed that, having seen her for that brief moment, he had never set eyes on her again.

Yet why should he?

After all, she was with the servants, whilst he was very much in the front of the house.

At the same time there was a definite mystery about her which he found intriguing and longed to solve.

Just why had she begged him so fervently not to mention he had seen her?

Why had she given him her right name and then corrected it quickly?

There had been a touch of fear in her voice and he had known by the look in her eyes that she was frightened.

Of whom or of what?

The questions kept coming into his mind.

THE BARBARA CARTLAND PINK COLLECTION

Titles in this series

A STEEPLECHASE
FOR LOVE

BARBARA CARTLAND

.com

Barbaracartland.com Ltd

THE BARBARA CARTLAND PINK COLLECTION

Dame Barbara Cartland is still regarded as the most prolific bestselling author in the history of the world.

In her lifetime she was frequently in the Guinness Book of Records for writing more books than any other living author.

Her most amazing literary feat was to double her output from 10 books a year to over 20 books a year when she was 77 to meet the huge demand.

She went on writing continuously at this rate for 20 years and wrote her very last book at the age of 97, thus completing an incredible 400 books between the ages of 77 and 97.

Her publishers finally could not keep up with this phenomenal output, so at her death in 2000 she left behind an amazing 160 unpublished manuscripts, something that no other author has ever achieved.

Barbara's son, Ian McCorquodale, together with his daughter Iona, felt that it was their sacred duty to publish all these titles for Barbara's millions of admirers all over the world who so love her wonderful romances.

So in 2004 they started publishing the 160 brand new Barbara Cartlands as *The Barbara Cartland Pink Collection*, as Barbara's favourite colour was always pink – and yet more pink!

The Barbara Cartland Pink Collection is published monthly exclusively by Barbaracartland.com and the books are numbered in sequence from 1 to 160.

Enjoy receiving a brand new Barbara Cartland book each month by taking out an annual subscription to the Pink Collection, or purchase the books individually.

The Pink Collection is available from the Barbara Cartland website www.barbaracartland.com via mail order and through all good bookshops.

In addition Ian and Iona are proud to announce that The Barbara Cartland Pink Collection is now available in ebook format as from Valentine's Day 2011.

For more information, please contact us at:

Barbaracartland.com Ltd.
Camfield Place
Hatfield
Hertfordshire AL9 6JE
United Kingdom

Telephone: +44 (0)1707 642629
Fax: +44 (0)1707 663041
Email: info@barbaracartland.com

THE LATE DAME BARBARA CARTLAND

Barbara Cartland who sadly died in May 2000 at the age of nearly 99 was the world's most famous romantic novelist who wrote 723 books in her lifetime with worldwide sales of over 1 billion copies and her books were translated into 36 different languages.

As well as romantic novels, she wrote historical biographies, 6 autobiographies, theatrical plays, books of advice on life, love, vitamins and cookery. She also found time to be a political speaker and television and radio personality.

She wrote her first book at the age of 21 and this was called *Jigsaw*. It became an immediate bestseller and sold 100,000 copies in hardback and was translated into 6 different languages. She wrote continuously throughout her life, writing bestsellers for an astonishing 76 years. Her books have always been immensely popular in the United States, where in 1976 her current books were at numbers 1 & 2 in the B. Dalton bestsellers list, a feat never achieved before or since by any author.

Barbara Cartland became a legend in her own lifetime and will be best remembered for her wonderful romantic novels, so loved by her millions of readers throughout the world.

Her books will always be treasured for their moral message, her pure and innocent heroines, her good looking and dashing heroes and above all her belief that the power of love is more important than anything else in everyone's life.

*"I have always felt that horses are not just beautiful
animals but are an integral part of romance.
I often imagine myself on a white stallion in the
arms of a handsome man riding away into
the sunset to an Eternity of love –"*

Barbara Cartland

CHAPTER ONE
1867

Helsa saw her father off in the family trap and then walked slowly into the garden.

She hoped that he would not find the journey to the woman who had sent for him too long or too arduous.

She knew that, when people were ill and turned to the Vicar for help, they had an infuriating habit of talking about themselves until he was exhausted.

The Reverend the Honourable Alfred Irvin was an extremely conscientious clergyman and he looked after the Parishioners in the village as if they were his own family.

As the younger son of the Earl of Irvindale, he had not joined the Army like his elder brother.

He was expected to take on one of the Parishes for which his father was responsible in the County of Surrey, and had therefore gone up to Oxford to read for a degree in history and theology and this he did so brilliantly that he was awarded a double first.

He was really, as his wife often said to him, far too able to be no more than the Vicar of a small Parish, but at the same time he was more or less living at home.

He enjoyed all the advantages of a great estate and a name which was revered over the whole countryside.

However, what had not been expected was that the Vicar's elder brother should be killed in the Crimean War.

The British Army had travelled out to the Crimea Peninsula more than thirty thousand strong to fight against the Russians in 1853, but very few had returned.

Neglected since the Battle of Waterloo, the Army was badly equipped and poorly led and owing to muddle and misinterpretation of orders at Balaclava, five hundred horses of the Light Brigade alone were killed or injured.

The Earl of Irvindale was totally broken-hearted at the death of his elder son and he died shortly before peace was signed.

Thus on the old Earl's death, his second son Alfred succeeded not only to the title but to the house and estate as well.

However, because he was so well known locally as 'the Vicar', he did not call himself the Earl of Irvindale as he was entitled to do.

Nor did he move from the Vicarage into Irvin Hall.

He realised for the first time that his responsibility was far greater and more difficult than he had anticipated.

Owing to the war and the fact that so many of their best workers left to join the Army, the estate had become neglected and unprofitable.

The Earls of Irvindale had been wealthy men for several hundred years, and their successors had carried on as if there were inexhaustible funds in the bank and they spent as much as they wished without a second thought.

As was usual with ancestral families, the Head, in this case the Earl, was responsible for all his relations, but the family estate had become impoverished because of the extravagance and disinterest of previous Earls.

And then the late Earl of Irvindale, handicapped by constant financial problems arising from the Crimean War and saddened by the death of his elder son, had found it impossible to keep the estate in good order.

It was now in a state of sad decline and producing very little income.

The Reverend Alfred Irvin was in despair.

How could he ever dispense what had become only a small income amongst so great a number of applicants?

"What am I to do, Helsa?" he asked his daughter with her long golden hair and shining blue eyes.

He thought as he looked at her how lovely she was.

If things had been normal, she would have gone to London as a *debutante* and would have then undoubtedly been a huge success in the *Beau Monde* who appreciated beauty whenever it appeared.

Instead of which she had to stay in Little Medwell and listen to the endless stream of complaints and requests that poured into the Vicarage every day.

But it was Helsa who thought up the bright idea of letting out Irvin Hall.

"Of course, dearest Papa," she had said, "you will never wish to sell anything that has been in the family for nearly four centuries. The Hall has been home not only for us but for everyone who bears our ancient name."

"No, definitely no," the Vicar replied to her almost angrily.

It had indeed passed through his mind that the only way to survive would be to sell *objets d'art*, but he knew only too well that virtually all the valuable objects at The Hall were entailed – for the son he did not possess.

He would be succeeded by a fairly distant cousin he had not seen for a long time.

But that was for the future.

For the present it was he and only he who could somehow contrive to keep the family alive.

"I think now we are at peace," Helsa was saying slowly, "more visitors from other countries will be coming to England. Perhaps we can find a rich man who wants to rent a large country house so he can entertain his friends."

Her father stared at her in astonishment.

"That had never occurred to me, but it could well happen and is certainly worth considering."

"What we have to do, Papa," continued Helsa, "is to notify the Agents in London who help foreigners to find accommodation whether it is in a hotel or a house."

"That is very clever of you, my dear. It would be a tremendous help if we could lease The Hall and save me from having to dispense with the few servants who are still there."

Helsa gave a little cry.

"You cannot think of doing so, Papa! The Cosnets had been with us ever since I was born. Robinson would, I know, rather die than leave The Hall, which he adores."

"I know!" the Vicar responded almost testily. "But unfortunately they have to eat and expect to be paid."

"That is why I am suggesting, Papa, that someone else does it for us. If we could find a suitable tenant even for a short while, things may well improve."

The Vicar sighed.

The last thing he wanted was to have to manage his estate as well as looking after the people who had always turned to him instinctively for help – not only his relations but all his Parishioners to whom he had been a guide and a comforter since they were born.

What was more, two of the other Vicars in villages round the estate had died or left and so he was responsible for not only running his own Parish but two others nearby.

It was more than enough to preach at three Services on Sundays and to baptise, marry and bury and at the same time to listen to their troubles was almost too much.

In fact he carried out all his duties extremely well and was consequently adored by everyone on the estate and in the neighbourhood.

Yet it was impossible for him to carry on doing so much for ever.

"Now if you will allow me, Papa," proposed Helsa, "I will write to two of these Agents in London who have advertised in the newspapers."

Her father gazed at her and she added,

"I am sure as they advertise in English newspapers, they also put advertisements into foreign ones. I think too that we should write to the Embassies and they may know of wealthy people from their countries visiting London."

"It certainly sounds a good idea," the Vicar agreed. "You must forgive me, my dear Helsa, for not thinking of it myself."

"It's a miracle, Papa, that you have time to think of anything except the people who hammer on our door day and night. Do you realise you have been out three times this week when you should have been sleeping to recover from the exertions of the day?"

Her father smiled.

"I have always thought it extremely unnecessary for people to die at night when they have the whole day to do it in," he had grinned. "I often think it is because they are left alone and find it easier to meet their God when there is no audience!"

Helsa had laughed.

Her father had a great sense of humour and she had often found herself laughing helplessly at his quips.

Equally she realised that no one could possibly do more for all those who turned to him in trouble.

It was so obvious to her that he was adored by those he served and the result was that they sent for him on every possible occasion and with every excuse however feeble.

"Now, when you come back from Mrs. Willow this afternoon, if she lets you off quickly, I suggest, Papa, that you go to bed and have a few hours sleep before dinner."

"What about my sermons for tomorrow?" he asked distractedly.

"You know perfectly well, Papa, you can deliver an excellent sermon without writing it all down. Just talk to the people from your heart and they will listen attentively. I sometimes think that because you enjoy writing so much, what you say goes over their heads."

"I know that, Helsa. Equally when I am writing a sermon, I often get carried away by my subject. It is only when I am reading it in Church that I realise that you are the only one in the congregation who will understand what I am trying to say!"

"I always enjoy every word of your sermons, Papa, but until you have more free time, I suggest you talk to the Parishioners about themselves and it's the only thing they listen to anyway!"

Her father laughed heartily, but he realised that his darling daughter was talking sense.

He had enjoyed teaching her enormously and it had delighted him when she grew older to find that Helsa was extremely intelligent. She wanted to learn more and more as he had when he was young.

Every penny he could spare went on buying books, which he read and discussed with his daughter and he often thought that other children would not have been advanced enough for such discourse.

The result was that Helsa at eighteen was not only outstandingly beautiful, as her mother had been, but she was also unusually intelligent and extremely well educated.

The Vicar had sat back in his chair before he said,

"Now you know I always listen to what you have to say to me. Tell me more about this idea of yours of letting out The Hall."

He was not feeling very optimistic, but he felt that he must give his daughter a free hand.

She wrote to every letting Agency in London which she thought might produce an interested client who would want, if only for a short time, to rent a large house in the country.

To her surprise and delight she received a number of encouraging letters in return.

Two people had arrived the next week to look at Irvin Hall, but unfortunately both of them had decided it was far too big for their requirements

Apart from anything else they would not have been able to afford the enormous staff that would be required if they rented The Hall.

It was useless for Helsa to try to maintain that they had managed with very few servants and she had to admit that all the State rooms were closed and so was one entire wing of the enormous house.

Then, by what Helsa believed to be an undoubted miracle, she heard from one of the largest Agents.

He wrote saying that he had received a request from a certain Lady Basset who was looking for a large house in the country in which she could throw large parties during the summer.

Helsa had felt when she first decided to advertise that it would be an advantage that they were near London.

She learnt when she visited the head of the Agency that Lady Basset wished to entertain – it would be mostly at weekends – in a very grand style.

Everything then moved so incredibly rapidly that Helsa really felt breathless at the end of it.

Lady Basset was willing to pay what she and her father thought was a very large rent for the house and the grounds.

It was all so exciting that they were half afraid the whole idea was just a mirage.

They were given instructions as to what was to be ready for her Ladyship's arrival and these multiplied day after day.

First she required a butler and four footmen – that was comparatively easy as Robinson had been at The Hall for so long and he could find exactly the sort of young men he would need in the village for the footmen.

Mrs. Cosnet, the cook, was thrilled to be told she could have two assistants and a scullion in the kitchen.

Her husband had always looked after the garden and he learnt that he had to make the lawns and flowerbeds round the house look as beautiful and well-kept as they had been when he was a boy – and it did not matter how many youths he employed to make this possible.

In fact the great house began to sound as if it was filled with bees and the walls seemed to vibrate with the activity inside them.

Helsa had gone to The Hall every day to see what more was needed and if the whole place could be ready by the time Lady Basset arrived.

It seemed an impossible task.

In addition her Ladyship had ordered a secretary to manage everything for her and it was just by luck that a former schoolmaster who had retired four years earlier was available.

Mr. Martin was an intelligent man and although he was now too old to teach children, he was delighted at the thought of being secretary and manager to Lady Basset.

He was made responsible for paying the wages of all the employees and took full control from the moment he arrived. As he knew everyone in the village personally, he helped Helsa choose the best.

"You cannot employ that man," he would say. "I remember as a boy he was extremely stupid and always did everything wrong. In fact I found him unteachable and I don't suppose he has improved much now he is older!"

Helsa had laughed, but at the same time she had accepted his advice and followed it.

Finding a suitable lady's maid for Lady Basset was, however, much more troublesome.

They were informed that her Ladyship possessed a great number of clothes and required someone who could wash, clean and iron them all, indeed someone who would make certain she always appeared smart and dressed as if she was 'a Queen'.

Mr. Martin and Helsa had both smiled at this last instruction, but equally they knew that this was one of the more difficult problems to be solved and in record time.

It was Helsa who had thought of the daughter of a doctor in one of the neighbouring villages.

Mary Emerson was one of her friends and she had always been adroit with her needle. In fact the things she made for local bazaars and for people at Christmas were outstanding.

"You can hardly expect Miss Emerson to take the place of a servant," Mr. Martin commented cautiously.

"It is only for a short time and anyway I think she would rather enjoy the experience," Helsa countered. "I will drive over later this afternoon and try to persuade her. Otherwise we may have to admit to Lady Basset that you cannot solve that particular problem."

"I hate being defeated," Mr. Martin retorted.

"So do I," Helsa agreed. "But you cannot always expect to find a fairy under a toadstool!"

Mr. Martin laughed, but he had agreed that Helsa should at once try to see if her friend would oblige, if only to give themselves time to find someone else.

When Helsa drove over to see Mary, she found, as she had expected, that her friend thought it would be a very amusing challenge.

"It will certainly be a new experience for me," she said. "I would love to see the really smart clothes I am told are worn in London. They are certainly something, Helsa dear, you and I will never be able to afford."

"Not unless we marry millionaires, but I do think the dress you are now wearing, Mary, is really lovely and I know you made it yourself."

"I found the material put away in the attic where it must have been lying for at least twenty years or more," replied Mary. "As it is very pretty I made it up for myself and it has proved most useful."

"It is very becoming," Helsa added, "and you are so brilliant with your needle. I often think, although perhaps I should not, that you are wasted on your village."

"Well, I cannot imagine anyone else will want me to sew for them – unless of course it is Lady Basset."

"Then you will do it, you will really do it!" Helsa cried. "You are an angel, Mary, and I cannot tell you how grateful Papa and I are. Everyone has been so kind and it is going to make such a huge difference to us, even if her

Ladyship only stays for three months let alone six, as they are suggesting at the moment."

"Are they really?" Mary remarked. "I wonder why she wants to rent The Hall."

"For big and important parties. We are having a tremendous job as you can imagine, getting all the State rooms cleaned up."

Helsa paused before she explained,

"My grandfather apparently never used them when he was old, because, as you may remember, he seldom had people to stay."

Mary nodded her head.

"So," Helsa continued, "they have remained there, waiting for this moment when they can burst back upon an astonished world."

"I always thought the State rooms were lovely," said Mary, "and I want to sleep in them myself."

Helsa looked at her reproachfully.

"Why did you not say so? You could have slept in The Hall for a night or two when you came over to stay with me."

"And cause all that trouble for one young girl. You know only too well what your grandfather would have said and to tell the truth I was so much happier with you at the Vicarage."

"I always loved having you, Mary, and at least we have been able to enjoy a good laugh, however difficult things have been."

"They have been difficult for us too," sighed Mary, "as soon as Papa gave up his practice. He was really not strong enough for it. If people were ill at night they had either to die or wait until the morning before he could get to them."

"Well, I am sure that if Mr. Martin has anything to do with it, he will make sure that Lady Basset pays for her comforts and an excellent lady's maid is surely the greatest comfort anyone could have."

"I have often thought that, and I am afraid, Helsa, that you and I are most unlikely to ever have a lady's maid of our own."

"We will just have to take it in turns to wait on each other – "

"That is certainly an idea," agreed Mary. "But if I ever marry, I would not want you to see too much of my husband. You are *too* lovely, Helsa, and I am certain, if we are ever allowed the chance of meeting exciting people, every man will fall in love with you as soon as you enter the room."

"Now that is the sort of thing I dream about," Helsa replied, "and which I know will never happen."

"But we must get married sometime – "

There was a silence before Helsa answered her,

"We will find it extremely difficult to find the sort of young men we read about in novels in this part of the country."

In fact she could not recall any young man being attentive to her or who had even found her pretty since the age of ten.

However, at this moment that did not matter.

What was important was that she had now found a lady's maid for Lady Basset.

"You must come over before she arrives," Helsa suggested, "and see that I have everything you require in the bedroom and the dressing room next to it. I expect she will bring masses of clothes with her."

"I do hope so as I very much want to see the latest London fashions and I would suppose that is where Lady Basset is coming from?"

"I am not quite certain," replied Helsa. "The letters I saw were rather vague, and Mr. Martin had the idea she has been abroad. That is why she has not come herself to view The Hall."

"Well, I hope her dresses are really smart," Mary said, "so that after she has left we can copy them. Then we can dazzle the stags in the Park and the birds in the trees!"

"I am certain they will be very appreciative," Helsa smiled.

They kissed goodbye after arranging for Mary to come over to The Hall at least two days before Lady Basset arrived.

*

In fact Helsa knew now as she walked in the garden that Mary should be arriving this afternoon as she had told Mr. Martin already that they would go up together to The Hall.

She walked round the small garden she had always tended herself just as her mother had done and beyond the lawn and the flowerbeds there was a herb garden that Mrs. Irvin had made almost perfect.

It contained, Helsa had always believed, a greater number of different herbs than any other garden she had ever seen or read about.

'I wonder if I could persuade Lady Basset to buy some of the creams I have made exactly the way Mama did?' Helsa asked herself.

She gave the herbs to poor people in the village for free and they never had the slightest idea that they might offer to pay for them.

Just occasionally when the richer folk in the County needed help, they would come to see her mother and consult her as to which herb would be best to cure their suffering, and naturally they paid for the creams she made for them.

Mrs. Irvin had always told them that if they were kind enough to pay for the herbs and creams, the money would go into the Church fund for those who were sick.

And her husband was exceedingly grateful for the help it gave him.

'Now things are totally different,' Helsa thought, 'but perhaps we can charge someone who is very rich for the creams. That will at least pay for the pot and the hard work I put into it.'

Then she laughed at the idea.

She thought that, just like the villagers, a stranger would automatically assume that anything that grew wild need not be paid for in hard cash.

She turned away from the herb garden to walk back to The Hall.

Then she saw Mary running towards her.

She was early and Helsa thought it would be fun to have time to talk to her before they went up to The Hall.

Then as Mary drew nearer she knew something was wrong.

"You are early, Mary," she said, as they reached each other.

"Oh! Helsa! Helsa! I have some terrible news to tell you. I know you will be angry, but I don't know what I can do about it."

"What has happened?" Helsa asked apprehensively.

"Papa has just had a letter from my grandmother to say that she is very ill and she needs him. He wanted to leave this afternoon, but I told him I must see you first."

Helsa drew in her breath.

"Do you mean you have to go with him?"

"You know that I must. Papa's eyes are too weak for him to drive alone. Also he gets tired very easily. As you know it is a long way to my grandmother's house and I have to take him there and, of course, bring him back."

For a moment Helsa could not speak and then she muttered,

"Are you really saying, Mary, that you cannot be lady's maid to Lady Basset?"

"I cannot see how I could leave Papa alone with Grandmama who only has one old servant to look after her. He said when he received the letter that she really ought to have someone in attendance night and day."

Because Helsa did not speak, Mary went on,

"He will try to find a nurse, but you know they are almost unobtainable. In any case very many of them are ghastly, they drink and generally upset the household."

Helsa knew this to be only too true.

There had been a host of stories of how badly the nurses had behaved, even when wounded men desperately needed their attention.

"I am sorry, I am so very sorry," Mary sighed, "but I have to go with Papa. I know I am letting you down, but there is really *nothing* I can do about it."

"No, of course you can't," agreed Helsa, "and I will find someone, somehow, to take your place."

"You know that we have thought of everyone in the neighbourhood and there was actually no one suitable. I am so devastated at letting you down, Helsa, but as Papa says, 'family must come first'."

"Yes, indeed it must, Mary," answered Helsa, "and I would feel the same if I was in your position."

"I knew you would understand," said Mary. "Now I have to hurry back and please, please forgive me."

"Of course I do. Don't worry I will find someone – even if I have to do it myself."

She was speaking lightly.

Then as she helped Mary back into the carriage she thought it was surely '*a true word spoken in jest.*'

She knew only too well that there was no one in the neighbourhood who could play the part of a lady's maid and certainly not in the way Mary could.

In fact, the only possible person capable of taking her place was *herself.*

As Mary drove off, Helsa waved until she was out of sight.

Then she wondered if she was being ridiculous.

She really could not play the part of a servant, even though a lady's maid's position was rather grander than a housemaid's.

She recalled when her grandmother and grandfather were alive that only a lady's maid was permitted to eat in the housekeeper's room – otherwise that prestigious room was kept exclusively for the housekeeper and the butler.

When guests arrived, their lady's maids, valets and coachmen were always well catered for and accommodated in the staff quarters.

The guests' servants would always eat their meals in the housekeeper's room and not in the servants' hall and Helsa had often laughed at this convoluted formula with her mother.

"It's a good thing we do not have to be so grand in the Vicarage," she would say. "Otherwise I suppose Mrs. Wilson and her husband would sit alone in the kitchen, while the other servants would have to sit in the scullery!"

Her mother had laughed.

But by the time she died, the number of servants at the Vicarage had been drastically cut down.

Yet it had always seemed there was more chatter and laughter coming from them than from the dining room.

Mary had driven away saying how sorry she was, but that she would be back as soon as she possibly could.

Helsa knew now she had the difficult task of going up to The Hall, and she would have to tell Mr. Martin that one of their most important servants for Lady Basset had unexpectedly been called away.

She was certain that, if Lady Basset was so rich, she would be extremely annoyed if there was no experienced attendant provided for her.

In fact it seemed rather strange that she would not be bringing her own lady's maid with her.

Why should she want to come to a strange house with nothing but strange servants?

Helsa thought there must be some reason for it.

Mr. Martin had already written to the Agents to say that everything was arranged as requested by Lady Bassett.

It took her less than five minutes to walk from the Vicarage across the Park and into the garden of Irvin Hall.

Because the vast house belonged to her family, she had often thought how lucky she was to have such luxury near her own small home.

She had always been permitted to take whichever books she wanted to read from the library – as long as she put them back in the same place.

It was difficult for her to realise that The Hall now belonged to her father, but no one knew better than Helsa that it was utterly impossible for them to live there.

How could they keep anything so enormous clean and pay the servants who would be required to do so?

All the same it was now her father's home and she had known it intimately ever since she was very small.

She let herself in through the front door. It was open and she well knew that it would not be locked until the evening.

Some of the newly engaged servants had already arrived and they would have established themselves, Helsa reckoned, in the most comfortable of the bedrooms allotted to them. They would also have been given a great number of instructions from Mr. Martin.

Helsa walked through the hall. The staircase rose on one side of it and there was a huge mediaeval fireplace on the other.

She glanced at the large array of Regimental Flags arranged on either side of the mantelpiece and they were, she knew, the flags collected by her many ancestors from the battles over the centuries they had fought in and won.

Her father had always spoken about the flags with pride and she wondered if Lady Basset would understand why they were there – even if they looked somewhat old and worn, she must be told how proud her family were of their provenance.

Mr. Martin was using the estate room as his Office. It had been there since The Hall had been rebuilt by the third Earl of Irvindale.

As Helsa knew it was piled with black boxes which contained the private papers of each successive generation as well as all the records of the income derived from the estate and notes of everything that had been spent on the house itself.

Mr. Martin, who was a good-looking man for his age, was writing at a desk in front of one of the windows.

When Helsa walked in, he asked,

"Is that you, Robinson?"

"No, it's me," Helsa replied, moving over the room. "I'm afraid I have bad news for you, Mr. Martin."

18

Mr. Martin rose to his feet.

"I thought that you would be along shortly, Miss Helsa, and that Miss Emerson would be with you."

"That is what I thought too. But, as I said, I bring you bad news."

Mr. Martin looked at her questioningly.

"You are not going to tell me that Miss Emerson cannot come? She promised she would."

"I know she did, Mr. Martin, and she is extremely distressed about it. But her grandmother has been taken ill and they have sent for Doctor Emerson. You know as well as I do that he cannot drive himself."

Mr. Martin gave a deep sigh and sat down again at his desk.

"What on earth are we going to do now?" he asked.

He spoke more to himself than to Helsa.

"I have been thinking about it," she replied, "all the way here. You know we simply could not think of anyone who could take on the job as lady's maid to Lady Basset. We were desperate until Mary said that she would take the position just for fun."

"She would have been excellent at it," Mr. Martin added rather gruffly.

"I know and she will come back just as soon as she can."

"We can hardly now ask Lady Basset after all this preparation to wait for her."

"I know," murmured Helsa.

Mr. Martin sat down on a hard chair near his desk and Helsa guessed, because he had not waited for her to sit down first, that he was feeling desperate.

He usually had extremely good manners.

"I have thought about what we can do," said Helsa. "In fact there is only one other solution to the problem."

"What is that?" Mr. Martin asked her with a note of despair in his voice

"That *I* must take her place."

Mr. Martin sat up in his chair and stared at Helsa.

"*You* would take her place?" he exclaimed. "But surely you cannot do that?"

"Why not?" she asked. "You know how important it is that Lady Basset should be pleased with the household when she arrives. I can imagine nothing more annoying for her than to be told that the lady's maid is unavailable and she will have to make do with one of the housemaids."

She glanced over her shoulder as she spoke to make sure that the door was closed and then in a lower voice she added,

"You know they all come from the village and have not the slightest idea how beautiful clothes should be kept and cherished. If they made a mess of them, her Ladyship would be furious."

"She would indeed," Mr. Martin agreed, "and Lady Basset might then refuse to pay what has already become quite a considerable sum."

"That is exactly why I must now take Mary's place. I will not be as good as her, but I promise I will be better than anyone else we can possibly think of."

She smiled before she added,

"Unless of course you have an angel tucked up your sleeve!"

"I am definitely not a magician, Miss Helsa. It is quite impossible for me to put my hand, as you might say, on anyone who could fill Miss Emerson's place as lady's maid except for yourself."

"That is exactly what I thought. I must, for Papa's sake, act the part of lady's maid until Mary is free or we can find someone who is really experienced."

"You know that is impossible, Miss Helsa. I can only say that it is extremely kind of you to do something you have certainly never done before. However, you are so clever that you will be, as we might say, 'well up to scratch'."

"Now you are just being complimentary, because you have got your own way and I have to convince Papa it is the right thing to do under the circumstances. But I am sure he will agree and we can only hope that Mary will not be away very long."

"I think it is wonderful of you, Miss Helsa, and if it was possible you know that I would do everything in my power to find someone else. But there is no one around here and I have always understood that a good lady's maid is essential for a *Lady of Quality*."

"Well, I only hope I am good enough and of course you must tell everyone in the household that no one is to tell her Ladyship who I actually am."

"I will do that, and they will obey me," Mr. Martin said, "for the simple reason they are grateful to have this particular job and are frightened it will not last very long."

He lowered his voice before he murmured,

"I am able to pay them more money than they have ever thought of earning in the past. Therefore they will not do anything I disapprove of."

"Then I will leave it all to you, Mr. Martin. I shall come in again tomorrow morning. I shall be sleeping in the nursery as we had fixed for Mary and I will not have anything much to do until her Ladyship finally arrives."

"All I can say," replied Mr. Martin, "is that you are an extremely sporting young lady, and your father will be extremely grateful to you."

He drew a breath before he finished,

"I only hope we do not have any more shocks like this one before the curtain goes up!"

"I was just thinking how lucky we are to have The Hall looking as it used to look when I was a little girl," Helsa sighed. "You have not forgotten to tell the gardeners to bring in plenty of flowers tomorrow?"

"Some flowers have been arranged already today. You might glance in the drawing room and see if they are exactly as you want them to be. I remember how glorious they looked in your grandmother's time."

"I thought everything in the house looked beautiful then," replied Helsa, "as it does now. I only hope and pray that Lady Basset is truly grateful for all the trouble we have taken for her."

"I expect, Miss Helsa, if she is as rich as we think she is, it is what she would expect to find everywhere she goes and therefore takes it all for granted."

"Of course, you are right – "

"In fact I have found in my long life," Mr. Martin carried on, "it is only when one loses something valuable that one realises just how special it was and how much it meant to one personally."

"That is very true, but whatever does happen I will always be exceedingly grateful to Lady Basset because the house is now looking so wonderful again."

She sighed before she continued,

"It is just as I remember it before my grandfather could not afford to keep it up and many rooms had to be closed."

"I am still hoping, Miss Helsa, that a real miracle will happen and your father will be able to live here and take his rightful place in the County."

"I have thought of that myself when lying awake at night. It would be so lovely for me to be the 'Lady of the Manor' so to speak."

Then Helsa gave a little sigh.

"You know better than anyone else, Mr. Martin, that it is something we cannot afford. Papa only laughed when I pointed out to him the other night at dinner that he cannot even afford to pay himself!"

"Your father is a very brave and saintly man, and when he does give up as Vicar who everyone turns to with their troubles, we will find it very difficult to replace him."

"I know that," Helsa agreed, "but I think what fun it will be to do the placing rather than be placed!"

Mr. Martin laughed.

"You have always got something smart to say, Miss Helsa, and only you would step into the breech as you are doing now."

"I can only hope that I do not fail. I must not forget from the moment I leave this room that my name is Mary. When I come here tomorrow, I am just another member of the staff and they must be very very careful not to give me away."

"I am sure they would not do so intentionally and I will make sure that they remember."

"As I shall be sleeping in the nursery," Helsa said, "I will feel I will not have to worry too much about myself. Nanny will be watching over me and making sure I don't make a mistake."

Mr. Martin walked towards the door with her.

As he looked at Helsa, he thought she was without exception the most beautiful young girl he had ever seen in his life.

At the same time he appreciated, perhaps more than anyone else in the village, how clever she was.

He reached for the handle of the door and said,

"Thank you, thank you more than I could possibly say for being so sporting and for saving the ship, because that is exactly what you have done."

"Cross your fingers," begged Helsa, "that I do not make a mistake and go crashing from my pedestal before I have really enjoyed sitting on it."

"Until tomorrow, goodbye to you, *Mary*!" replied Mr. Martin.

"Goodnight, *sir*," Helsa answered him.

They were both laughing as she walked down the passage towards the front door.

There was still no one in the hall and so Helsa let herself out and closed the door behind her.

As she walked down the drive she told herself this was an adventure – at least it was something new and very different.

As she crossed the bridge over the lake, she thought it was a predicament that had never happened to her before.

Perhaps in such a humble position she might learn something that would be extremely interesting and even in some unexpected way that she could not really imagine, exciting and above all, exhilarating.

'It is just what I need at the moment,' she thought. 'We have all been too depressed and dismal for too long.'

As she walked on, she thought the birds in the trees were singing as if they understood her.

There was a lightness in her heart that had not been there before.

CHAPTER TWO

Helsa was up at The Hall long before they expected Lady Basset to arrive.

She immediately went up to the room that had been her grandmother's to find that everything was clean and tidy and the room itself looked extremely inviting.

She had mentioned to Mr. Martin that there must be flowers in every room and she noted with satisfaction that her instructions had been carried out. Cosnet had picked armfuls of beautiful blooms and they had been extremely well arranged, Helsa thought, by the new housekeeper.

She was an elderly woman, a certain Mrs. Walters, who had lived in the village all her life, but she was rather better educated and came from a superior family to most of the villagers.

Helsa inspected the wardrobe and the dressing table so that she would know exactly where to put Lady Basset's belongings when she began the unpacking ritual.

Then she walked downstairs to visit Mr. Martin in his Office.

As she came in, he rose to his feet.

"You are forgetting who I am," Helsa said with a twinkle in her eye. "You would not stand up for the lady's maid!"

"I might if she was attractive enough!"

Helsa laughed.

"I think that very unlikely. From what I remember of lady's maids staying at The Hall when my grandfather and grandmother gave parties, they were mostly all middle-aged disagreeable women and they invariably offended the housemaids, who then complained to my mother."

"Everyone in the village took their complaints to your mother, Miss Helsa, and she always had a kind word for everyone."

"That is indeed true. I am sure Mama would think what we are doing here is a great joke. But she would help out with the details we have forgotten."

"I hope you have forgotten none," said Mr. Martin. "If you have, it is my head that will fall, not yours!"

Helsa laughed and sat down at the desk.

"What I have really come to ask you," she began, "is if you know anything about Lady Basset? I really don't want to put my foot in it by being rude about wherever she comes from or saying anything which would make her feel I was being overfamiliar."

Mr. Martin spread out his hands.

"To tell the truth I know very little about her, Miss Helsa. I did ask the Agent to send me any information he could, but I think he is in the same position as we are. He just knows her by name and has not even set eyes on her."

"So we don't know if she is old or young, pretty or ugly. But if she wants to entertain so lavishly, she must be attractive in some way."

"Well, all I can tell you," added Mr. Martin, "is that Robinson and the kitchen staff would be very disappointed if they had only one lady to do everything for."

"So would I and I would want to put out for her the prettiest dresses she possesses and, with the help of the real Mary, copy them if I can!"

Mr. Martin chuckled.

"I might have guessed, Miss Helsa, that you were not going to waste your time in any way. I expect you are already contemplating rifling The Hall's library more than you have done already."

"I have listed every book I have ever taken," Helsa insisted, "and so has my Papa. I would assure you that we are very careful of what we own."

She sighed wistfully,

"It would be so wonderful if Papa could live in this house as his ancestors did and afford to keep it as clean and beautiful as it looks at the moment."

"'*If wishes were horses, beggars could ride*'," Mr. Martin quoted. "At the same time I hope and pray, Miss Helsa, that one day your dreams do come true."

"I have a feeling somehow they will. I cannot think how. But that is what makes all this such an adventure. If we are not prepared to face every problem when it occurs, we will get nowhere."

"You are a very wise young lady. Now let me get on with my current task which is to determine how much I can charge Lady Basset for the staff working for her."

Helsa started.

"Do charge as much as you can!" she cried. "When Lady Basset departs, we may not be so lucky in finding someone else as rich to rent The Hall. Then everyone in the village whether they are working here or not will be very disappointed."

"I will do my best and no one can say more!"

Helsa smiled at him and left the Office.

She thought as she walked down the passage how lucky they were to have Mr. Martin in charge.

She realised, just as he had been in the school, he would be strict in having everything exactly as it should be and at the same time he would be liked and respected by everyone who worked for him.

Even the naughtiest little boys at the school liked him despite the fact they were always being punished, and she remembered that the elder boys and girls really enjoyed the lessons they had received from Mr. Martin.

Her father said they were very lucky to have such an excellent village school and as many of the boys and girls sang in the choir he knew them all well.

Helsa went into the kitchen and found Mrs. Cosnet, as she had anticipated, in somewhat of a flutter.

"It's all so difficult for me, Miss – H – "

She started to say 'Helsa' and then as she caught Helsa's eye, added quickly,

" – Mary."

"What is wrong, Mrs. Cosnet?" asked Helsa.

"It's just that I don't know what 'er Ladyship will fancy and 'ow can I plan a meal if the dishes I've chosen are the ones she most dislikes?"

"I can see that makes it difficult, Mrs. Cosnet, but I am sure that as soon as she does arrive, Lady Basset will tell you which her favourite dishes are."

"I only 'opes so, but I'll be ever so upset if any of those I've chosen for 'er comes back untouched."

Helsa knew of old that she was very sensitive about her cooking and so was as consoling as she could be before she left the kitchen for the garden.

Cosnet had done wonders in the short time he had been given with three youths working on the weeds and Cosnet himself was cutting still more flowers for the house as Helsa congratulated him on what he had done already.

Then she went into the hall to find Robinson.

He was standing at the front door looking out down the drive through an avenue of ancient oaks.

Just as Helsa reached him, he exclaimed,

"*Here she comes*!"

Without replying Helsa looked in the direction of his eyes and saw that coming up the drive was a carriage drawn by four horses.

She could see that there was another carriage, if not two, behind it.

She realised as lady's maid she should not be in the hall and so she ran upstairs to stand on the landing waiting for the first carriage to reach the courtyard.

She could just glimpse the horses and thought that they seemed exceptionally fine and despite the fact they had come all the way from London, they travelled up the drive at a very slick pace.

She squeezed herself back against the side of the wall so that she could see but not be seen.

Below one of the footmen was now running down the steps to open the door of the first carriage.

A man stepped out first and then he turned to help a woman alight.

As they walked towards the house and the carriage moved away, Helsa watched the two other carriages move forward.

She had only a very quick glance and then she was mesmerised by watching the woman walking up the steps.

She was being met at the front door by Robinson.

He was bowing politely and Helsa heard him say,

"Good afternoon, my Lady. May I welcome you to Irvin Hall."

"I presume you are the butler," the woman said in a firm and well educated voice.

Robinson bowed.

"I am, my Lady."

Peeping down, Helsa could now see Lady Basset a little more clearly.

At first all she was aware of was a large profusion of ostrich feathers and then as the wearer moved her head, she saw the glitter of diamond earrings.

Then Robinson led the way across the hall towards the drawing room.

Now Helsa could really see Lady Basset.

She was, she thought, certainly good-looking if not alluring and there was no doubt that she was elaborately dressed in what must have been most expensive clothes.

Then Helsa was aware of the man following her.

He was tall, dark-haired and extremely handsome and she wondered if, in fact, Lady Basset had a husband and this was he.

Then another couple appeared in the doorway.

The woman was smartly dressed too, but she was much older than Lady Basset appeared to be and the man with her was at least in his fifties.

His hair, when he next handed his hat to one of the footmen, was going grey.

As the second couple walked towards the fireplace, Robinson reappeared after showing Lady Basset into the drawing room.

Bowing politely to them, he showed the newcomers the way and they had hardly disappeared from view when four more visitors appeared at the front door.

Helsa saw that they were all young men.

Smartly dressed and obviously in their twenties or thirties, they were laughing and talking among themselves.

One of them was pointing to the flags.

"That is what you should have brought back from the Crimea, Harry," one piped up.

"I never had any chance of getting anything but a tummy ache from the filthy food we had and a streaming cold from the mud we slept on," was the answer.

Then before Helsa could hear the response to this, the four men disappeared from her sight.

She reckoned that Robinson was showing them into the drawing room.

Fortunately she had noticed that he had arranged a grog table for the drawing room, which had certainly never been there in her grandfather's time.

She had, however, made no mention of this grog table, as she thought Robinson very likely knew more than she did about the requirements of Socialites.

She was certain now that the newcomers, especially the men, would expect to be offered a glass of champagne on their arrival.

The whole idea seemed to her very dashing and not at all in keeping with the quiet life that had been lived at The Hall ever since she had been a child.

She had often stayed at The Hall when her father and mother had gone away on holiday or there had been repairs at the Vicarage.

Then the house had been very quiet and if the Earl entertained, it was usually his more elderly neighbours in the County who regarded him with awe and Helsa always thought they lowered their voices a little when they spoke to him.

Now already she could hear loud laughter coming from the direction of the drawing room and she felt that

Lady Basset's visitors were going to be very different from those of earlier days.

Of course when her father and his younger brother were young they had had their friends from Oxford to stay, and her father had related to her how much they enjoyed racing their horses across the fields.

There had been a steeplechase once a year in which other riders in the neighbourhood could join in.

But Helsa had not been born when that took place.

When she had stayed at The Hall, sleeping in the night nursery even when she was too old to have a nanny, everything had been very quiet and sedate.

Her grandparents always retired to bed at precisely ten o'clock and for the first time she now wondered at what hour she would be expected to be still on duty to help Lady Basset undress before she retired.

When she went into the bedroom, she looked round and wondered if there was a comfortable chair where she would be able to doze and still hear Lady Basset coming upstairs before she actually entered the room.

One of the housemaids called Betty had been told to be ready just in case her Ladyship required a bath before dinner.

She told Helsa what was happening downstairs.

"Two more gentlemen and yet another couple's just arrived," she muttered breathlessly, "and Mr. Robinson's runnin' backwards and forwards to open bottle after bottle of champagne for 'em!"

"I wonder what time they are expecting to have dinner," Helsa enquired of Betty.

"I 'eard from Mr. Robinson, "that it be ordered for eight o'clock, but 'er Ladyship says that some of 'er guests might be a bit late."

"You mean there are more to come?" Helsa asked in astonishment.

"Two more to come from London, I understands. One of 'em be a Lord someone or other, I didn't get his name."

It was certainly a bigger party, Helsa thought, than she expected and she hoped Mrs. Cosnet would not panic.

At least she had enough staff in the kitchen to help her – the only difficulty was if she had enough food.

One thing, however, was really very consoling – there were plenty of bedrooms.

Never in her lifetime had she had known The Hall have half its bedrooms occupied, even at Christmas with relatives to stay.

When she thought it all over, her grandparents had lived quite simply without a great number of servants.

She could not help wondering whether Mr. Martin would have to engage additional staff, unless of course the visitors had brought their own servants with them.

She was told later that three of the gentlemen had brought valets with them and the older lady her own lady's maid.

There was one issue that Mr. Martin had been firm about and Robinson had fully agreed with him, and it was that Mary Emerson as lady's maid to Lady Basset should take her meals in her own room – and one of the footmen would take them up to her.

It would be a considerable mistake for her to be in the housekeeper's room where visiting servants could think that she was different from them and gossip might reach the ears of Lady Basset.

Helsa felt glad that she had agreed to Mr. Martin's arrangements and she would not have to sit down with a plethora of strange servants who might easily be curious about her and then make Lady Basset feel curious too.

'I suppose that I should really disguise myself with a pair of ugly spectacles,' she reflected, 'or make myself look older in some way!'

Then she told herself that a servant was a servant, and it would be doubtful if Lady Basset or anyone else in her party would be interested in anything except their own friends.

It was, however, rather strange to think that there were so many young gentlemen in the house.

She was sure if her father was here, he would enjoy their company even though they were much younger than he was.

*

Helsa was waiting obediently in the bedroom when Lady Basset finally came upstairs.

She was laughing and talking to the elderly couple who had followed her into the house.

Robinson had led the way upstairs and then handed the guests over to Mrs. Walters and she was in the process of showing them to their rooms.

Helsa thought she must have been surprised at the number of gentlemen there were compared to the number of ladies.

But she heard her intoning most respectfully,

"And this one, my Lady, is your room where all the Countesses of Irvindale have always slept for generation after generation."

"I hope they won't haunt me," Lady Basset quipped as she walked into the bedroom.

"This is Mary, my Lady, who'll be looking after you," added Mrs. Walters, indicating Helsa.

Lady Basset nodded to Helsa and murmured,

"I hope she does it well."

She did not shake hands with her as Helsa knew her mother and grandmother would have done.

Instead she walked across to the dressing table and commented,

"I wonder if there is enough light here for me to see myself clearly in this mirror. If there is one thing I really dislike, it is being economical where lights are concerned, especially in my bedroom."

There were three candles on each side of the mirror and two small candelabra by the bed.

There was also a large chandelier hanging from the ceiling and as far as Helsa could remember it had never been lit during her grandmother's lifetime. She gazed up at it anxiously wondering if the candles had been renewed or maybe they were just for decoration.

As if she had asked the question aloud, Lady Basset rambled on,

"I will manage alright for tonight, but tomorrow I want that chandelier lit when I come up to dress for dinner and blown out when I have finished dressing."

"Very good, my Lady," replied Helsa, speaking for the first time. "Will your Ladyship be requiring a bath this evening?"

"I had one this morning and there is really not time now, but I would like to wear one of my prettiest gowns, so I hope you have unpacked them."

The luggage had been carried upstairs soon after the guests had arrived and Mrs. Walters had instructed one of the housemaids to unpack Lady Basset's trunks to save Helsa from doing so.

She had, however, watched where each gown had been hung so that when she pulled open the wardrobe, she would know which one Lady Basset required.

"The green one will suit and I will then wear my emerald jewellery with it," she demanded imperiously.

Lady Basset started to undress and Helsa was at once impressed with the silk underclothes she was wearing, all trimmed with the most expensive lace.

Her gowns too had appeared magnificent when they were taken from the trunks and hung up in the wardrobe.

When she helped Lady Basset into her green gown, she recognised that it must have cost a fortune and it had obviously been designed by a Master hand.

She suspected, although she had no real knowledge of his work, that it had been designed by Frederick Worth, the top dress designer in France and his gowns were the joy of the Empress Eugenie herself.

When Helsa looked closely again at Lady Basset, she realised that she was not as old as she had expected.

In fact she doubted if she was more than thirty.

She was not exactly beautiful, but had an attractive face and she made the very most of herself.

Her hair had a touch of red and on her instructions Helsa fixed a bandeau of large emeralds on it.

She mused that nothing could look smarter or more magnificent and there was a necklace of emeralds to match it together with earrings and a bracelet.

Finally Lady Basset put a very large emerald on her ring finger.

She did not speak while she was being dressed and then she expected Helsa to arrange her hair.

Fortunately Helsa had often done her mother's hair for her, especially when she was going to a smart party and she managed, she thought, to make Lady Basset's hair look extremely pretty although she did not say so.

In fact Lady Basset merely gave her orders rather sharply as if her appearance bored her, but at the same time she intended to have exactly what she wanted.

Finally when she was dressed and Helsa had knelt down to put her shoes on her feet, she looked at herself in the long mirror on the door that led into the boudoir.

"It is just impossible to see myself," she muttered crossly, "with so little light. Make sure the chandelier is always lit in future, Mary, together with the smaller lights which are to remain alight until I come to bed."

"I will see to it, my Lady," replied Helsa.

Lady Basset looked at her as if for the first time.

"Who did you work for before you were engaged for me?" she enquired.

Helsa was ready for this question and, as she hated lying, she responded,

"I have been at home, my Lady, because my mother died and my father had no one to look after him."

"Oh! I suppose you are glad to have this position to bring you in a little money."

"Yes, of course, my Lady, I am very grateful."

"I understand that the Earl and Countess who lived in this house are dead and that the new Earl cannot afford to live in it."

"That is so, my Lady."

"It is certainly a very large house and on the whole well-furnished. In fact anyone coming here would, I think, be somewhat impressed by the house itself and no doubt the grounds."

Helsa did not know how to answer her, so therefore she did not speak.

"I only hope," Lady Basset went on, "the food is as good as I was promised it would be and the dining room has the right amount of silver."

"The silver is very fine, my Lady, and it has been in the Irvin family for generations and is reputed as being one of the foremost collections in England, just as the picture gallery contains some superb masterpieces."

"That is what I want to hear," replied Lady Basset. "Therefore anyone coming to this house for the first time would be impressed by what they see?"

"I am sure that they would," Helsa agreed. "It is just unfortunate that the present Earl cannot afford to live here."

"He is the Head, I am told, of a very ancient family, but I understand that there is no chance of my meeting him while I am staying here."

"I don't think so, my Lady."

Helsa was wondering where this conversation was leading and why Lady Basset appeared so inquisitive.

"Now please tell me, Mary," she continued, "what was the previous Earl like and is there a portrait of him anywhere in the house?"

"Yes, my Lady, there are portraits of the previous Earl and Countess in the dining room. You will see them when you go in to dinner. They are on either side of the marble fireplace and the other pictures are of the previous Earls of Irvindale down the centuries."

"That is just what I want to know, Mary. You must tell me more about the Irvin family while you are dressing me tomorrow morning."

She was walking towards the door when Helsa said,

"I expect you would like me to stay up to help your Ladyship undress."

"No, no! I much prefer to manage myself. But leave everything ready for me and then wake me tomorrow morning at half-past eight."

"I will do so, my Lady."

Lady Basset took one further look at herself in the long mirror and, as Helsa held open the door for her, she swept out onto the landing.

As she did so, a gentleman came out of the master bedroom along the corridor – he was the tall good-looking one with whom she had arrived.

Lady Basset stood waiting until he joined her.

"I hope, my dear Duke, you found everything to your satisfaction," she asked him.

"Everything – and I have been most impressed with what I have seen so far of this delightful house."

"Unfortunately we have not been able to use it for some considerable time," Lady Basset added. "Therefore you must forgive me if things here are not yet as perfect as I should like."

"I am sure your magic fingers make everything you touch turn into gold," declared the Duke. "Only *you* could have a dream house like this waiting for us unexpectedly."

"That is exactly what I wanted you to say," Lady Basset smirked.

She slipped her arm through his and they walked down the stairs together.

Helsa watched them, feeling that the conversation she had just overheard could not be true.

How was it in any way possible that Lady Basset was pretending that The Hall was her own house?

She had never seen it until she arrived an hour ago.

What was the reason for such deception?

Helsa felt that she knew the answer.

It was the Duke she wished to impress.

It was the Duke who had been placed in the master bedroom.

The same Duke she was now walking downstairs with and telling him that the house belonged to her.

Undoubtedly she would make herself related to the portraits she had just been told were on either side of the marble fireplace.

Helsa drew in her breath.

This was a development she had not anticipated and it was certainly very perplexing.

Equally she could not understand how Lady Basset really thought she could get away with such an obvious pretence.

First she tidied away Lady Basset's clothes she had worn on her arrival and then she turned down the bed and left everything ready for her. She laid one of her pretty diaphanous nightgowns trimmed with real lace on one of the chairs.

It was then she remembered there was a connecting door between this room and the master bedroom where the Duke was sleeping.

It must have been made clear to Mr. Martin that although Lady Basset, being unmarried and the hostess of the house party could have been in the master bedroom, the Duke was to occupy the best room available.

She obviously did not know the Duke that well as she was addressing him as '*my dear Duke*'.

Yet the way she had taken his arm and the note in her voice when she spoke to him told Helsa that the Duke meant something special to her.

Then she thought that Mr. Martin must know more about all this than he had told her, so having finished in the bedroom, she went down the backstairs that were not far from the dining room.

She could tell from the noise that they had already gone in to dinner.

She had been right in thinking Mr. Martin would be in his Office and she had already learnt that because he was nervous in case things might not go right, he himself was staying in the house, while his wife remained in their house in the village.

Helsa opened the door of the Office and Mr. Martin looked up from his desk.

"I thought I would find you here," she began.

"I hope everything is alright," Mr. Martin asked her anxiously.

"Everything as far as I know, but many more guests have arrived than I expected."

"Fortunately I had been told that there might be an unlimited number of guests," said Mr. Martin, "so I warned Mrs. Walters."

"You did not warn me and I was astonished – "

Helsa sat down on the chair next to the desk.

"A strange thing has just happened, Mr. Martin, and perhaps you will have an explanation for it."

"What is it, Miss Helsa?" he asked quickly.

"When Lady Basset left her room, a gentleman she addressed as 'my dear Duke' was just coming out of the master bedroom. As they walked downstairs, I distinctly heard her imply to him that this was her own house, but she had not been able to live in it for some time."

There was silence for a moment and then as she looked questioningly at Mr. Martin, he remarked,

"I hoped that you would not find this out, but I did know about it before she arrived."

"You knew – but you did not tell me?"

Mr. Martin smiled.

"You know quite well that I did not expect you to be here and there was therefore no reason to tell you what might upset you. I am quite sure it would have remained a secret to Miss Emerson as she is not as bright as you are."

Then Helsa responded smilingly,

"It is no use trying to flatter me. But do tell me the truth, Mr. Martin. Why is she then pretending to own The Hall? It seems to me so extraordinary."

"It seemed so to me when I was told it by the man who came down from London to see if the house fulfilled her Ladyship's requirements."

"Which it did, but why does she have to pretend to own it?"

"No explanation was given to me. I was only told that her Ladyship was looking for a distinguished ancestral house that had always been in the possession of aristocrats. When Irvin Hall was then offered to her, she accepted it with alacrity, alleging that she was a direct descendant of a previous Earl of Irvindale."

"But I have never heard of her in my life," Helsa protested. "You know as well as I do that Papa has been most meticulous in keeping the family tree up to date. I assure you there is not a single mention of anyone called Basset anywhere."

Mr. Martin looked embarrassed.

"The manager of the Agency who found this house for her, Miss Helsa, told me in confidence that Lady Basset was anxious to pose as being related to one of the most famous names in the country. In fact she had turned down quite a number of large houses simply because she did not consider their owners aristocratic enough."

Helsa laughed.

"Well, I suppose there is no need for us to mind her pretending to be a relation. It just seems to me to be a very strange way to behave."

"Very strange indeed," Mr. Martin agreed. "But as you rightly say, it can do no harm and I thought that it was something you would never know as you were not at all likely to meet Lady Basset."

"Of course I should have wanted to meet her, but I didn't think she would be particularly interested in meeting me, unless she went to the Church and was impressed by Papa."

Even as she spoke she knew by the expression on Mr. Martin's face that he did not think Lady Basset would be that impressed by the village Vicar – unless she learnt that he was really the Earl of Irvindale.

"But so far there have been no other puzzles," she added, "and I suppose that Lady Basset's claim to own the house is to be kept from the other servants."

"I think, to be frank, Miss Helsa, she does not know that there are any servants in the house who were here with your grandparents. In fact when the Agent came down to inspect the house, he thought there were just two caretakers in residence and I saw no reason to argue the point."

"So what he was making sure of," Helsa ruminated, "was that Lady Basset could not then be accused of lying, whatever she may tell her guests."

"I suppose that is true enough, but you must agree, Miss Helsa, that we have arranged an amazingly high rent for this house, and it would be such a tragedy if we upset her Ladyship and she walked out without paying it."

Helsa gave a cry of horror.

"Of course it would be and Papa is counting on the money to carry out restoration on the estate. Once we can start, I am very confident that we shall have excellent crops once again and produce something to sell."

"I am well aware of the current financial situation and therefore the longer Lady Basset stays here and the more demands she makes for extra servants and a number of other matters she mentioned to me tonight, the more she will have to pay."

"I am only grateful you are here to extract it from her, Mr. Martin, but I think it is a mistake for Papa to find out that she is telling lies. You know what he feels about people who lie."

"It is just unfortunate, Miss Helsa, that you have big ears," Mr. Martin teased her.

Helsa giggled.

"I have been accused of many things, but not that before!"

"I had the idea, until you came in to see me," Mr. Martin added, "that no one would know of her Ladyship's pretence and I have no intention of telling anyone."

"I would hope not. And I promise not to tell Papa. It was just rather unfortunate that I should overhear, the very moment she arrived, that she is playing a part as if on the stage. I am sure that all her guests are expected to do is to applaud her!"

"Of course, and it is something they will naturally do. Robinson has told me that she has brought extremely expensive gifts for all of them. He was only aware of that, because as they were so valuable, she told him to put them in the safe."

"She must be very very rich," commented Helsa.

"I can only hope that is the truth and not another deception."

Helsa gave a little cry.

"Oh, don't frighten me! I really think that it would break Papa's heart if the tide has not turned as he believes and again we have to consider every penny we spend and leave so much undone that ought to be done."

"I do understand. But all I can say, Miss Helsa, is that you can trust me. We can only hope that we will sail through the storm to prosperity with the help of God and no one else."

"That is what I hope and will certainly pray for, Mr. Martin. Now I think it is time I went to bed. I am sorry to have kept you up for so long."

"I will not go to bed until everyone else has done so. I want to be quite certain that the coachmen have been properly looked after and there is no trouble in the stables."

"You are wonderful, you think of everything. We are so very grateful that we have someone as robust as you to manage all this."

Mr. Martin rose to his feet and smiled at her.

"I might have guessed that I could not keep a secret from you, Miss Helsa. Actually I have worried quite a lot about Lady Basset's plan to pose as a descendant of some great ancestral family. To tell the truth, when I heard that this was what she wanted, I put the price she had to pay for renting The Hall and estate up considerably!"

"Oh, Mr. Martin," Helsa exclaimed, "you really *are* amazing! I only wish we could tell Papa. He would think it so funny!"

"But it is his business as Vicar," Miss Helsa, "not to encourage lies and deception!"

Helsa put up her hands.

"I was only teasing – and I promise I will not say a word to Papa. Anyway I have no wish to upset him."

"Nor have I. Now do go and rest and don't worry. Leave the worrying to me. Tomorrow may bring us more problems."

"I am praying there will be none – but I cannot help feeling that this makes the game even more exciting than it is already."

"As long as it does not get out of hand," Mr. Martin cautioned.

Helsa walked to the door and as she opened it, she looked back.

"Goodnight, Mr. Martin, and thank you for being so marvellous. I think Papa and I are so lucky to have you."

She did not wait for his reply, but closed the door behind her and ran upstairs.

CHAPTER THREE

As soon as Helsa was free the next morning, she hurried back to the Vicarage.

She had left a note for her father to say that she was going to The Hall and thought that, as there were so many guests arriving and everyone was consequently in such a fluster, she should stay the night.

She was determined not to let him know the real reason why she was staying there.

As she walked towards the Vicarage, she wondered how she could convince him that she was still needed at The Hall.

She should not have worried – her father was very pleased to see her, but as usual he was extremely busy.

"I have a wedding today, my dear, in Upton, which you know is on the border of the estate, and a christening late in the afternoon in the other direction."

"Oh, Papa, it is too much for you!"

He smiled at Helsa.

"I will manage. Now tell me how they are getting on up at The Hall."

"Everything so far is going quite smoothly, Papa. The only problem is that there are far more people staying than Mr. Martin expected."

"Well, I imagine there is plenty of room for them, my dear, but you must help him all you can."

"That is exactly why I am staying up there," Helsa replied. "As you know, the staff, especially the new ones, are not used to people from London. Mr. Martin and I are terrified they will make too many mistakes."

"Well, you can only do your best, no one can do more – "

Helsa knew he was not really listening to her and she was grateful for that mercy.

If he had asked her direct questions, she would not want to lie, but it made it much easier that her father was so immersed in his own duties.

She saw him off on his rounds.

Then, as she was about to return to The Hall, the old groom, George, who looked after her Papa's horses, ambled into the kitchen looking a little sheepish.

"I hears, Miss Helsa," he began, "there be some fine 'orses a-comin' 'ere for the steeplechase."

"*Steeplechase*?" repeated Helsa. "I did not know we were having one!"

"They be talkin' about it in the pub last night and sayin' it be a difficult ride, but there's never been such fine 'orses in the stables as there be right now."

This was all news to Helsa and she considered that Mr. Martin should have told her.

Having chatted to George for a short time and then to Bessie, who cooked for her and her father, she started back across the Park.

She could not help wondering if George had got it all wrong, as he usually did.

Maybe there was really no steeplechase and no fine new horses in the stables.

Equally she wondered for the first time how Lady Basset intended to entertain so many gentlemen.

She was thinking in the night that there were now nine of them, including the elderly gentleman, and only three ladies. It was a party that she would have enjoyed herself, but she thought wistfully she was never likely to host one.

What interested her more than anything, however, were the horses – they had managed to keep two horses at the Vicarage with George to look after them.

Her father rode one and she rode the other, but her horse was sadly growing old.

She had no intention of allowing him to be 'let' out with the Hall. He stayed out in the paddock where he was quite happy until she wanted to ride him, but she thought that he must have missed her these last two days when she had not been able to go and see him.

There was no time at present, but she told herself she must slip down to the Vicarage again as soon as it was possible, not only to make her father happy but to go and pat her beloved mount.

He was called 'Golden Arrow'.

It was a name she had read about years ago in the newspapers when a horse of that name had won a classic race and it had always stuck in her mind.

She had always wanted to own a horse she could call 'Golden Arrow'.

'Perhaps one day,' she reflected, 'I will be able to ride horses that George would call 'fine'. Then my horse will be worthy of being described as one that travels very swiftly.'

When she reached The Hall, it was not quite eleven o'clock and she thought there would be no chance of Lady Basset requiring her services until nearly luncheon time.

She had dressed her this morning almost in silence and said nothing unusual, yet Helsa had felt instinctively that she was annoyed about something.

She only hoped it was nothing that concerned the household, but she thought it would be a mistake to ask her any questions.

Now she wondered what the guests would be doing after breakfast and she was almost sure if they had brought horses with them, they would be out riding.

If there really was to be a steeplechase, she could understand why Lady Basset had asked so many gentlemen and so few ladies to her party, unless of course she wished to remain the 'Belle of the Ball' without any competition.

Because she was so curious, Helsa approached the stables from the back.

She passed through a small clump of trees and over a piece of waste land and when she drew nearer, she could hear no guests in the stables as if there were, they would be talking to the grooms.

She was quite right and when she turned into the stable yard, there was no one to be seen.

Only as she pushed open the door to the first stable did she see that there were several new horses that had not been there before.

The groom rubbing down a particularly fine stallion was also a stranger.

As she then stopped, he touched his forelock.

"Good morning," said Helsa.

"Mornin', ma'am."

"That is a magnificent horse you are attending to," she remarked to the groom. "Who does it belong to?"

"To 'is Grace the Duke of Mervinston."

"He is certainly a very beautiful animal – "

As she spoke, she pushed open the door of the stall and slipped in. She patted the stallion and recognised that he was more majestic than any horse she had ever seen.

Certainly he was far superior to any animal that had been in the stables before.

"Where are the others?" she asked, hoping that she had not made a mistake and there were no others.

"They be out bein' ridden by them gentlemen as be staying 'ere at the big 'ouse," the groom replied.

Then before she could ask another question he said,

"His Grace brought two 'orses with 'im. One 'e be breakin' in. It'll be givin' 'im a tough time this mornin'!"

"I expect he is a very good rider," Helsa muttered.

She had no idea whether he was or not, but she was curious about him.

The groom grinned.

"'E be one of the very best, and if 'e don't win yon steeplechase tomorrow, I'll eat me 'at."

"That will undoubtedly give you acute indigestion," giggled Helsa, "but I hope he does."

"'E'll do it all right, ma'am, and you just mark me words, 'e'll show 'is 'eels to them other gentlemen."

Helsa smiled at him.

She then let herself out of the stall and walked back to The Hall.

She went in through the backdoor and straight into Mr. Martin's Office.

"Good morning, Miss Helsa," he greeted her as she entered. "I was wondering what had happened to you."

"I went back to see Papa and then George told me that they are holding a steeplechase! You did not tell me."

"I did not get the chance. When you left me to go and wait on her Ladyship, I was informed when she arrived that there would be twelve guests in the house which I had not expected."

Helsa realised he was feeling quite indignant as he went on,

"An expert on steeplechases is also arriving today to arrange one for the gentlemen who are here. Then I was told that horses for the event would be coming in late last night and that those who were bringing them would require accommodation."

Helsa laughed before she replied,

"Oh, poor Mr. Martin! It must have been a shock for you!"

"I am getting used to it and fortunately The Hall is quite big enough to house an Army if necessary. So the newcomers, after they had put their horses in the stables, slept in the East wing."

"If they are all going to be here every night," Helsa cried, "you will need one or two more housemaids to make their beds if nothing else."

"I have thought of that already and I have got two women coming from the village who, quite frankly, I had previously not thought good enough to work here."

Helsa laughed again.

"It is no use being too particular. I was astonished when I saw so many gentlemen arriving yesterday with her Ladyship, but now I know the reason."

"It is certainly a new way of entertaining and one which will amuse your father when he hears about it."

"I have just been to see Papa. He is very busy and fortunately did not ask me too many questions."

She felt as if some of the tension disappeared from Mr. Martin's eyes and then she continued,

"He quite understands that you need me here and was not at all upset that I have to stay away from home."

"Well, thank goodness for that. I was afraid that he would insist on your going home and I was wondering if Mrs. Walters would be able to cope in your absence."

"She is doing very well, but I should not suggest asking any more of her. I will try to see Papa some time during each day so that he does not believe it his duty to come to find me."

Mr. Martin threw up his hands.

"Oh, don't let him do that! I am sure that the Vicar would be extremely upset at you pretending to be a lady's maid. He would also be perturbed that we have had to tell quite a number of lies."

"I do agree with you, Mr. Martin, that it would be a great mistake to worry Papa. Now I had better go upstairs and see if her Ladyship's room is exactly as she wants it."

She paused before she added,

"To tell the truth I am just longing to see the rest of the horses. The ones in the stables at the moment are truly magnificent."

"If I was you, I should go whilst they are having luncheon or dinner," Mr. Martin suggested.

She climbed up the backstairs and along a corridor to the room occupied by Lady Basset.

She could see that the housemaids had cleaned and tidied the room perfectly and she could not find fault.

Helsa wondered if there was anything she ought to do to the gown that Lady Basset had worn last night. She had hung it up in the wardrobe and found there was not a crease in the material and it was actually too over-trimmed for any part of it to need ironing.

Helsa had always heard that Frederick Worth put more trimmings on his gowns than any other couturier had ever done and she thought now it was a distinct blessing for the poor overworked lady's maid!

She was closing the door of the wardrobe when she heard a noise behind her.

Turning round she saw a man coming through the door that led into the master bedroom.

For a moment she just stared at him. Then she realised from the way he was dressed that he must be a valet.

"Can I help you?" she asked.

"I was just going to ask you – " he replied.

He spoke well, but with just a slight inflection in his voice that told Helsa he was indeed a valet.

She walked nearer to him.

"What can I do for you?"

"I expect you're the lady's maid to the Mistress of the house. I was hoping to find a key to this door."

As he spoke he glanced at the communicating door.

As Helsa followed his eyes, she saw that there was a lock on the door, but no key.

"I do suppose," she responded, "there must be a key for it somewhere, but actually I have never seen it locked and it may have been lost."

She remembered a time when her grandmother had been ill and she had been sitting beside her bed when her grandfather had come through that door which led directly into his own room.

"I thought I heard your voice, Helsa," he had said, "and I am glad you have come to see your grandmother. She is finding it rather lonely now she is tied to her bed."

"I have brought her some herbs," she remembered replying. "You have lots in your own garden, but Mama thinks these would heal Grandmama quicker than yours."

Her grandfather had laughed.

"I know your mother thinks that," he said, "and the whole village believes trustingly in everything she gives them. At least they will do your grandmother no harm."

"They will certainly not hurt her," she had replied.

Her grandfather had then patted her shoulder as he reached the bed.

"You are a good girl to try and help anyone who is ill, as your mother does. It is something you must keep on doing when you grow older."

"I promise you I will do so," she had smiled at him.

Then he had gone back the way he had come.

Whilst Helsa had been looking back into the past, she realised that the valet was looking closer at the lock – as if there was a way of making it work without a key.

Then he said with a sigh,

"There must be lots of keys in this house. Where can I find some to try in the lock?"

"You must ask Mr. Martin," Helsa answered him. "I am sure he will have a collection somewhere."

"I'll do that," the valet replied, "and if you ask me these connecting doors are a nuisance and people should be made to use the proper door to a bedroom with a key in it."

He spoke almost angrily and then Helsa countered,

"I cannot think why you are worrying. I am sure, as her Ladyship sleeps here, no one will think of entering His Grace's room except through the door in the passage."

The valet looked at her and then he smiled,

"You're so young, and I'd suppose they keep you innocent in these outlandish parts. But you take my advice and if you're put in a bedroom that has a door like this, you keep it locked."

"But why? I don't understand."

Helsa looked perplexed.

The valet gazed at her.

"Well, I'll tell you something else. When there's a handsome man like the one I has to look after, it's always wise for him to lock his door at night."

"Do you mean people might slip into his bedroom and steal his possessions?" asked Helsa.

The valet laughed again.

"They're more likely to steal *him!*" he guffawed. "I'll tell you another thing. I has to keep the women from running after him as if they were a swarm of bees."

Helsa looked at him wide-eyed.

"You learn a lot about people if you valets them as I does or sews up their dresses as you do, and if you ask me, you're too pretty and too young for the job."

"I don't understand," persisted Helsa. "I am quite certain that no one would go into His Grace's bedroom in the night without knocking on the door. Then, of course, he could refuse to let them in."

The Valet stared at her as if to make certain that she really did not understand what he was implying.

Then he continued,

"It's a mistake for you to know too much. But just take my warning. If you're sleeping in a room which has not got a key to the door, you'll have to bar it, so no one'll get in and surprise you when you're asleep."

"I should be very frightened if anyone came into my bedroom when I was asleep," said Helsa. "If you think that might happen to your Master, I will go down now to ask Mr. Martin if he has a key for the door. But I honestly think it is quite unnecessary."

She thought the valet looked at her in a strange way as if he thought she must be pretending to be so naïve.

She could not imagine why on earth Lady Basset should want to enter the Duke's room – unless she wished to give him something to help him sleep or if she thought something had been forgotten – perhaps like biscuits by the bed or extra candles.

Almost as if he knew what she was thinking, the valet was watching her and then he remarked,

"You're far too pretty for this sort of job. Is there nothing else you could do, like teaching children at school or sewing clothes at home for your mother?"

"My mother is dead and I am only being a lady's maid at present because it was so difficult for Mr. Martin to find so many servants in this part of the County."

The valet nodded as if he understood.

"Well, I don't know where you're sleeping but you shut your door tonight and lock it. Then if anyone tries to come and say goodnight to you, he'll not be able to get in."

Helsa laughed as she could not help it.

"There is no one likely to do that, and certainly not where I am sleeping, but thank you for trying to protect me from feeling frightened."

"I think, now I've talked to you, it's more likely you'd be shocked," said the valet. "But I can promise you I have to guard His Grace and if you don't find me a key, I'll have to find something heavy to put against this door."

"I will go and talk to Mr. Martin right away."

Helsa hurried down the stairs, thinking as she went that the valet was being very fussy.

She could not imagine why he should suspect Lady Basset of wanting to go into the Duke's bedroom after they had all retired to bed.

Mr. Martin was not in his Office and Helsa guessed he might have gone to the stables to see if everything had been properly prepared for the new horses.

So she then walked out of the back door and was heading for the stables along a narrow path bordered with clumps of rhododendrons, when she saw a tall handsome man wearing riding clothes walking towards her.

She came to a standstill.

As he reached her, he said,

"I think I have taken a wrong turning. I was trying to find the way back to the front door."

"This way only leads to the kitchen," replied Helsa, "and if you go back a little way and turn left, the path will lead you to the front of the house."

She suddenly realised that she was speaking to the Duke – the man she had watched last night from over the banisters.

For a moment he did not turn away, but asked her,

"Are you staying in the house? I did not meet you at dinner last night."

"No, I am lady's maid to Lady Basset."

"*Lady's maid*!" the Duke repeated in astonishment. "But you do not seem – "

He stopped as if he thought that what he was about to say might seem rude, so instead he enquired,

"Do you belong to this part of the world?"

He was thinking as he asked her the question that he had never seen anyone quite so lovely and he certainly did not expect the beautiful girl facing him to be a servant.

"Yes, I live near here, and I only came in to oblige, because the household is very short-handed."

"I thought there must be an explanation for it," the Duke remarked. "What is your name?"

This took her by surprise.

Without thinking she replied, "Helsa". Then added quickly, "but everyone calls me Mary."

"I much prefer Helsa," the Duke mused. "I think, if I am right, the name has some special meaning."

Helsa smiled at him.

"It actually means, '*given by God*', and that is why my father and mother chose it for me after I was born."

"It is a lovely name and so why do you spoil it by using another one?"

Helsa thought quickly.

"Most people do find it difficult to pronounce and even more difficult to spell, so Mary is easier when I am working like this."

"I can well understand that," the Duke said a little doubtfully. "Now, unless you are going back to the house, can you show me where I went wrong?"

"If you will come this way, Your Grace."

She moved so that he could walk beside her.

And then he asked her,

"Where are you going? To your home?"

"No, I was going to the stables. I saw your horse this morning and I think he is absolutely superb. He is one of the finest stallions I have ever seen."

"That is just what I think myself, but the other one I was riding this morning will be almost as good when he is properly broken in."

"Do you do it yourself, Your Grace?"

"I do it when I can, and it is what I enjoy. Besides I think a horse always has a special attachment to the person who breaks him in."

"That is what my father has always said. I do feel myself that if you possess that certain affinity with your horse, he is far easier to control than if you are a stranger to him."

"Of course you are right," the Duke agreed.

By this time they had reached the yard where the Duke had taken the wrong turning and Helsa stood still.

"You go down that path," she told him, pointing the way to the front of the house.

"Thank you. I am most grateful, Helsa, and I hope I will meet you again."

It suddenly struck her that she should not have met him in the first place and it would be a mistake for him to talk about it.

"Please," she asked him quickly, "don't tell anyone you have seen me or that we have had this conversation."

The Duke looked surprised.

"Why ever not?"

"Because there are reasons as to why I should not be here and certainly not talking to one of the guests."

He did not answer and Helsa looked up at him and persisted,

"Please, *please*, forget this has happened."

"I will not forget it, but, since you have asked me, I will not speak of it to anyone."

Helsa smiled at him.

"Thank you so much, Your Grace, and don't forget that is a promise."

"I will not forget – "

He walked away and Helsa turned and went back into The Hall.

She had suddenly thought it was very stupid of her to have even considered going to the stables so late in the morning, as those who had been riding would obviously be returning for luncheon.

'I must remember to keep my place,' she scolded herself. 'Otherwise if Papa hears about it, he will be angry and it would be even worse for us if Lady Basset refused to pay the rent.'

So she therefore retraced her steps to Mr. Martin's Office, sat down and waited.

She had been there five minutes when he entered.

"Hello Miss – M-Mary," he began stammering over his words. "I hope that all is well in the house."

"All is well on the domestic front, but you must tell me more about the steeplechase."

"I was told that Lady Basset had arranged it before she left London and a steeplechase expert had already been engaged to organise it for her and the horses were on their way."

"Do you mean she brought all the horses especially for her guests?" Helsa asked him.

"From what I gather, but when she asked the Duke to stay, he said he would bring his own horses with him. It was this that put the idea into her head that there should be a steeplechase."

"It is all quite bewildering!" exclaimed Helsa. "But equally it must be wonderful to have so much money that you can arrange a huge event at a moment's notice without giving a thought to the expense, or to the extra people you will have to employ to carry it out."

Mr. Martin laughed.

"I thought that myself – and naturally I will charge extra for the stabling of so many extra horses. They have mostly come with their grooms, but I am quite certain that we will require more help in the stables."

"That is exactly what I want to hear, Mr. Martin."

She suddenly remembered why she had come to see Mr. Martin in the first place.

"His Grace's valet has just asked me for the key of the communicating door between his own room and Lady Basset's."

"The key! I should have thought that it was the last thing they wanted!"

Then, as if he had spoken without thinking and felt embarrassed, he said rapidly,

"But if that is what His Grace requires, I must find the key for him. There is a box of keys here that belong to a great number of rooms in this house, but I have no idea which. If you will take it to him, it will certainly keep him busy finding the right one."

He went over to one of the shelves in the room and produced a box heavy with keys.

Helsa looked at them and laughed.

"If he is going to try all these, it is going to take him a long time. As I said to him, I cannot imagine anyone will want to use that door when they can reach the Duke quite easily from the corridor."

Mr. Martin was about to say something, but then he pursed his lips together.

"I will take the box up to the valet," said Helsa. "I will tell him if there is nothing in it that fits, he had better ask you if another lock can be fitted on the door."

She was silent for a moment before she added,

"And if it makes a mess, it will undoubtedly annoy her Ladyship."

"I agree it may annoy her, but it may also annoy her even more – if the valet *does* find the key he is seeking."

"I cannot imagine why," Helsa replied. "She cannot possibly want to go into the master bedroom except to see that it is tidy and the Duke has everything he desires. She can do that through the door on the corridor."

"Yes, of course she can," he agreed hastily. "Just give the valet the box of keys and tell him to return what he does not need to me here in this Office."

Mr. Martin appeared to be in a hurry and Helsa felt that he had work to do and perhaps she was preventing him from doing it.

"I will take it up to the man at once," she offered.

She had already reached the door when Mr. Martin remarked,

"I should not tell her Ladyship that the Duke's valet requires the key for the communicating door."

"Why ever not?" Helsa enquired.

"Because I think it would annoy her considerably. Therefore please just do as I say and that is another matter we should all keep our mouths shut about."

"I cannot think why, but if you think so, I will do as you suggest, Mr. Martin."

Mr. Martin did not reply, so Helsa went out of the Office closing the door behind her.

She had no idea that after she had gone Mr. Martin wiped his forehead with his hand, wondering distractedly what the next obstacle would be.

Upstairs she entered Lady Basset's room.

She next decided to open the communicating door to see if the Duke's valet was in the master bedroom.

There was no sound of voices, so she thought that the Duke was not present – he would be with Lady

63

Basset in the drawing room drinking champagne before luncheon.

Very gently just in case there was someone in the room, she pushed open the door.

To her astonishment she found that she was unable to open it although it was not locked and then she realised that something heavy had been placed against the door on the other side.

'I cannot think why he is making such a fuss about this door,' she told herself again.

Going into the passage she knocked lightly on the door that led into the master bedroom.

There was no reply, so she pushed the door open and was not surprised to find the door was unlocked.

She put the box of keys inside the room and then went back to Lady Basset's room.

She noticed at once a strong scent of her Ladyship's best perfume. She had smelt it when she had dressed her last night and this morning Lady Basset had used the scent spray before she put on her gown.

'I am sure that the gentlemen downstairs will find it very attractive,' she reflected.

Then she wondered what the Duke had felt.

Because he was so tall and handsome she was quite certain there would be a great many women running after him and making themselves beautiful just for him.

Then suddenly, and she thought she must have been very silly not to have thought of it before, it occurred to her that perhaps Lady Basset was running after the Duke!

That was the reason why his valet wished to lock the communicating door between their rooms.

'Why did I not think of that?' Helsa asked herself.

Then she knew it was because Lady Basset, while being very rich, was not a young girl and it had therefore never occurred to her that she could be pursuing the Duke.

'I must be very stupid,' she then told herself, 'but if she is a widow and wants to marry again, who could be a more prestigious and desirable husband than a Duke?'

Because she had never dealt with such a problem before, it took her a long time to consider it and then to answer her own questions about it.

She stood in the window gazing out into the garden and as she did so, she saw people coming out onto the lawn beneath her.

The three gentlemen she had caught a glimpse of as they had arrived last night were there and Lady Basset in a very attractive gown was walking beside the Duke.

She was talking animatedly as they moved towards the fountain.

Cosnet had eventually managed to make the ancient fountain work after it had remained silent and empty ever since Helsa could remember.

The gentlemen bent over the carved marble basin and looked down into the water which filled it, as if they expected to see goldfish swimming there.

As they did so Lady Basset and the Duke, who had their backs to Helsa's window, stopped too.

The Duke threw back his head to look up at the water that was streaming out of the top of the fountain and then Helsa saw Lady Basset move a little closer to him.

She put her hand very softly but caressingly on his arm.

Lady Basset was indeed pursuing the Duke in the way that his valet had told her many women pursued him.

What was more, Helsa thought, she now knew the real reason why Lady Basset had rented The Hall and was pretending it was part of her own inheritance.

It was an effort to impress the Duke and make him think that her blood was the equal of his.

Of course she wanted to marry him.

She wanted to become a Duchess.

It all came clearly into Helsa's mind.

At the same time she thought how foolish she had been not to realise it before and because Lady Basset was so rich, she had been thinking of her as being old.

It had never struck her for one moment that all this scheming and searching for a superb ancestral background was designed to make an impression.

Not on the Social world in general, but on one man – *the Duke* – who could make her his wife and a Duchess.

CHAPTER FOUR

Helsa was woken abruptly by the maid coming in to pull back her curtains.

She turned over and stretched as the maid piped up,

"There be complete pandemonium downstairs, Mr. Robinson'll tell you about it, miss."

She was gone before Helsa could reply.

She jumped out of bed quickly wondering just what could have happened.

It was very important that today of all days things should run smoothly when they ran the steeplechase.

She was dressed and had brushed her hair when she heard Robinson come into the nursery with her breakfast and she guessed that he had something urgent to tell her.

She walked from her bedroom into the nursery and asked,

"What has happened, Robinson?"

"A real mess it is, Miss Helsa. It's something that would never have happened in his Lordship's time."

"What would not have happened, Robinson?"

"They've just found that some trees've fallen down in the strong wind and made the course dangerous so that the steeplechase has to be postponed."

"*Postponed!* But it was all arranged!"

"It were," Robinson agreed. "But the man who's running it says he won't be responsible till the trees have

67

been removed. Although the men be working at it now, it won't be cleared before late this evening."

"But surely they can ride past that particular bit of the course – "

Robinson shook his head.

"It'd be a mistake for them to do it the wrong way and have an accident, especially with His Grace's horses."

This was true and Helsa knew it would be a disaster if either of them was injured.

"So what is happening, Robinson?" she asked.

"The Steeplechase'll now take place on Monday as tomorrow's Sunday – it'd shock the village if they raced on the Sabbath!"

That was absolutely right as Helsa knew and her father would certainly disapprove.

She gave a little sigh.

"Well, if it is on Monday, it should be all right for everyone, providing the guests do not have engagements elsewhere."

She was wondering as she spoke if the Duke would stay on or take his magnificent horses away.

Almost as if Robinson was reading her thoughts he added,

"Her Ladyship first made quite sure His Grace'll stay and all the other gentlemen have agreed they'll stay on too."

Helsa gave a sigh of relief.

Then Robinson went on,

"What's happening now is the man who be running the steeplechase – I can't remember his name – is going to put up fancy fences in the paddock and they are going to have a jumping competition for everyone in the house."

Helsa smiled.

"That is better than nothing and will keep them busy."

"That's what I thinks too. Since the steeplechase is postponed, no guests from outside the house-party will be coming for luncheon today. But they'll all be coming on Monday."

He left the room without saying anything more.

Helsa smiled to herself as she sat down at the table.

She well knew that Robinson and the older servants hated any alterations to their plans and that there would not be so many people for luncheon as expected would surely upset the cook.

She felt thankful that the Duke was staying on, as if he had left, Lady Basset might have terminated her tenancy abruptly and that would have been disastrous.

Helsa could not help herself being worried about the money that had been spent on servants, food and the steeplechase. If Lady Basset then refused to pay the bills, it would be exceedingly embarrassing if not disastrous for her father and all their plans.

'Whoever they work for,' she reflected, 'Papa still thinks they are 'our people' and it is our duty to help and protect them.'

However, according to Robinson everything would still be alright.

The Duke would stay and that meant all the other riders would wait for the steeplechase on Monday.

And by that time Lady Basset might well have the gentleman all this palaver was all about in her clutches!

*

The gentleman in question – the Duke – was at this moment talking to the organiser of the steeplechase whose name was Watson.

"It be no use, Your Grace," he was saying, "I can't give the 'off' to any man who might be injured, apart from a horse having to be destroyed, because I made a mistake in allowing the race to take place."

"No, I do agree that would be wrong," replied the Duke. "Equally it means everything being postponed until Monday and it would be far better if you could have made the course avoid that particularly dangerous place."

"You know what them woods be like, Your Grace. They've been neglected for years and there be boughs of trees apart from trunks fallen all over the place."

The Duke would have spoken, but Watson went on,

"I tried to follow the path through the woods which I were told has been used for generations, but no one has cleared up after the gales when they comes in the winter."

"I can understand, Watson, but at the same time it is most irritating not only for those who are staying here at The Hall, but for those who have brought their horses from other parts of the County."

Watson smiled.

"Your Grace'll see that they'll all turn up alright on Monday. Her Ladyship's giving out a number of first-rate prizes and when a steeplechase be paved with gold, so to speak, everyone wants to take part in it!"

The Duke chuckled.

"I'm sure that's true, Watson. So we must all wait until Monday."

"What I've been a-thinking, Your Grace," Watson added, "is that you and the gentlemen staying at The Hall could still have a good afternoon's sport. I've arranged for jumps to be put up in the paddock where they used to be years ago."

The Duke was now listening attentively to Watson and he then continued,

"It'll be a bit like a Racecourse for all them young gentlemen and if I get a dozen or so jumps up by lunchtime you can try your horses out on them. The ground's clear and firm enough for there to be no accidents."

"That is a very good idea and something I will look forward to. One of my horses I have not yet tried out on jumps. But if, as you say, you will have some challenging jumps for us in the paddock, it will make the afternoon most worthwhile."

"I'll certainly do my best, Your Grace."

Watson walked away smiling.

He was actually thinking that this alteration to the programme ought to mean many more gold sovereigns in his pocket than he had already counted on.

*

A little later Helsa was sent for by Lady Basset and she found her rather surprisingly in a cheerful mood.

At first she could not understand why Lady Basset was not upset at the change of plan and then once again Helsa told herself she was being foolish.

Lady Basset had no wish for the Duke to leave The Hall too soon and now he would stay two extra days until the steeplechase had been run.

Her Ladyship chose one of her prettiest gowns from Paris to wear and she left her bedroom smiling and in a better temper than she had been ever since she had arrived.

Helsa was so relieved she was not in a rage about the change in plan and hurried down to the kitchen.

"Here we be preparin' for at least thirty or more for luncheon," Mrs. Cosnet wailed, "and now I hears they're to be turned away to come back on Monday. The food won't last that long, I'll be tellin' you!"

"I would not be too sure it will not be eaten today," replied Helsa. "I heard that the jumps were only to be for those staying on in the house, but I have a feeling when the others arrive for the steeplechase, it will be difficult for her Ladyship to send them away. You will find, I am sure, that they will come into luncheon."

No one apparently had thought of this eventuality and Mrs. Cosnet was placated and she was smiling by the time Helsa left the kitchen.

Her next visit was to Mr. Martin.

"Nothing ever goes smoothly," he moaned, "but I am surprised that her Ladyship is not as angry as I thought she was going to be."

Helsa glanced at the door to make sure that it was closed.

"I have the idea," she confided, "that her Ladyship is delighted because it means that the Duke will stay with her at The Hall longer than she might have expected."

Mr. Martin stared at her and then his eyes twinkled.

"I think you're right, Miss Helsa. It had not entered my head, but now it seems highly probable."

"Think it out, Mr. Martin, but I don't know what you are going to do with them all on Sunday."

"I am quite certain none of them will want to go to Church," he mused, "but one just never knows and I am slowly getting used to surprises when I least expect them!"

"So am I, Mr. Martin, but I am quite determined to watch the steeplechase whatever happens, whether it takes place today, Monday or even Sunday."

"Your father would have a stroke if it happened on Sunday. It is such a pity you are not taking part in it, Miss Helsa. It would cause a sensation if the steeplechase was won by a woman!"

"That is why I would love to win it, but frankly I know that Golden Arrow is now too old."

She left Mr. Martin and went back upstairs, wishing that she could go to the stables and visit the horses again.

But she knew that was where it was likely most of the gentlemen would go after breakfast.

She was not mistaken.

*

The Duke was the first to rise from the breakfast table and say he was going to see his stallions.

"I also want to take a good look at these jumps," he murmured. "It would be a mistake for them to be too high – and disappointing if they are too low."

The others agreed with the Duke and then professed how much they looked forward to a jumping competition in the afternoon as there was no steeplechase.

"How can we work it out?" one of them demanded. "Three times – or should it be four – over the jumps. And we must time it rather than risk several of us trying to take a jump at the same time."

"You are quite right," the Duke came in. "We must definitely time it. I will go and talk to that man Watson, who is organising the steeplechase and the jumps and see what he suggests."

"He is supposed to be extremely good at this sort of thing," one of the other guests remarked. "I did ride in one he arranged in the North, but the weather was ghastly and it was not as enjoyable as it could have been."

"In other words, you did not win," one of the other guests chortled.

"I think I distinguished myself by coming in last!" was the reply.

The Duke had already left the dining room and was on his way to the stables.

He looked first at his two horses. The best one had already been well brushed down and bridled by his groom before the news came that the steeplechase was called off.

"We're that disappointed, Your Grace, and it's no use sayin' we're not," the groom told him. "Masterpiece were all ready to carry Your Grace to the winnin' post!"

"Well, I am sure he will win on Monday," the Duke replied. "In the meantime, Brown, they are going to have some jumps erected in the paddock and I would like you to have a good look at them and make sure they are not too high. It is always a mistake to overtax a horse, especially when it is new to its rider."

Brown nodded to show that he agreed.

"They were settin' up some of the jumps yesterday afternoon and they looked well done to me, though I didn't take too much interest in 'em at the time."

"*Yesterday afternoon*?" the Duke quizzed. "But I understood it was only decided this morning after the wind last night that the steeplechase was to be postponed and the jumps put up instead."

"Yes, that's right, Your Grace, that was what I were told."

The Duke thought it somewhat strange.

Since the steeplechase was to be such an important event, surely the local grooms should have been attending to the course rather than putting up jumps in the paddock.

However, it was undoubtedly an *'ill wind that blew nobody any good'*.

As the Duke inspected his two stallions, he thought it would be quite amusing to spend the afternoon jumping.

*

He had concentrated on his horses ever since he had come into the title and had been able to extend his stables and purchase the very best horseflesh.

He was determined not only to own the best horses to ride but also to race.

His father had a racing stable, but he had not been particularly interested in it and when the older horses died or were put out to grass, he did not replace them.

The Duke was running two horses at Royal Ascot this year, both were exceptionally fine thoroughbreds and although he had paid a great deal for them, it had certainly not been a waste of money.

In point of fact the Duke took so much interest in horses that his family teased him, complaining that as they could not induce him into marring a young and pretty girl, he would have to marry a horse!

"I am sure I would be far happier with a horse than with most of the women you have tried to force me up the aisle with," he volunteered the last time one of his aunts was pleading with him, as they all were, to produce a son and heir.

"You will be twenty-eight at your next birthday, Victor," she had scolded him, "and I *do* think it is time you settled down and had a family."

"I cannot understand, Aunt Sylvia, why you must always be in such a hurry," the Duke had answered her. "Every man is entitled to 'sow his wild oats'."

His aunt pursed her lips.

"But you have been sowing yours for too long," she retorted, "and as far as I can make out you spend more on horses than on any woman, however beautiful she might be!"

"The young women my family press on me might well be pretty, but after I have been with them for even five minutes I know I should be bored stiff with them in five months, let alone years!"

"Oh really, Victor, this is too ridiculous," his aunt exclaimed. "Of course the young girls are not particularly intelligent when they are *debutantes*, but they grow older and wiser as the years pass. It is your job as a husband to teach them not only about love but about the matters that interest you."

"Very well then, it's horses," he persisted. "But the last girl you tried to pair me off with had hands that would have destroyed a carthorse!"

His aunt sighed.

"It was a big mistake to bring that particular girl to your notice," she agreed. "But she did come from a very good family and her blood is as blue as ours, and you must admit that is *so* important."

"It may be very important to you, Aunt Sylvia, but personally I find anyone who cannot ride, who has never read a book and who is not at all interested in architecture or history, extremely boring, however blue her blood."

His aunt had held up her hands in despair.

"Honestly, Victor, you expect too much. Of course young girls are like that, but they grow into those attractive and amusing married women with whom I understand you continually associate – "

"*Not* continually, but there are certainly one or two young ladies in the *Beau Monde* I have found extremely amusing. However, to be perfectly honest, Aunt Sylvia, I have no wish to take the place of their husbands, who often find themselves sadly neglected."

"Nonsense, Victor. They may have other interests than their wives. What I am trying to point out to you is that those wives were once boring *debutantes*. The years changed them or rather their husbands did and that is just what you will have to do yourself sooner or later."

"The mere idea of it depresses me and I can tell you one thing, Aunt Sylvia, I have no intention at any time of being pushed into an 'arranged marriage'. So you and my other relations can just stop thinking it possible."

Once again his aunt threw up her hands.

"You will not listen to us, Victor, but we are indeed frightened that sooner or later you will get caught by one of these amusing temptresses you spend your time with."

She paused for breath, then went on,

"A scandal in the family would be appalling and as you well know, a divorce is just unthinkable, but a husband might fight for his rights and where will you be then?"

"I will think of an answer when it happens – "

Then he strolled out of the room leaving his aunt almost in tears.

"He is hopeless," she said to another member of the family the next day. "I try to talk sense into his head, but he will not listen. If we are not careful I am quite certain he will either run away with one of those dreadful tigresses he is always with or remain a bachelor because he prefers his horses!"

She was exaggerating and the family then laughed at her, but at the same time they had all tried to make the Duke aware of his duty and he would not listen to them.

As he had so often told himself, he would never be pushed, shoved or coaxed into matrimony, just because he was Head of an old and distinguished family and indeed extremely rich.

His father had thought it would be a great mistake for any young gentleman to have too much to spend and had therefore deliberately kept him short of money until he came into the title.

There were so many adventures he now wanted to undertake that it took him several years to try all of them.

He travelled as he had always longed to do, but had previously been prevented because his father thought it a waste of time.

He journeyed to many different parts of the world that few people had ever visited.

He came home to find that his house in London had been done up exactly the way he wanted it and the stables at his country house had trebled in size – so all he had to do now was to fill the empty stalls.

He spent a great deal of money at Tattersall's and because it amused him, he travelled all over the country to visit other people's stables, especially when they had some interesting horseflesh to sell.

*

The Duke had been fully aware that Lady Basset was pursuing him from the moment they had first met.

But as it was nothing particularly new and, as she was not outstandingly beautiful, he had therefore not paid any special attention to her.

Then she had spoken to him about a steeplechase.

Because her house was near London and he had just bought two outstanding thoroughbreds – Masterpiece and Samson – the Duke had agreed that he would compete in her steeplechase.

She had told him it would be the most difficult of all courses and the best arranged steeplechase that had ever taken place.

He rather doubted this, until he heard that Watson, a well-known authority on steeplechases had been engaged to organise it.

He had then accepted Lady Basset's invitation.

She told him it would be taking place at her family home, Irvin Hall in Surrey.

He had suggested one or two gentlemen she might invite, because they were rivals of his and owned stables that were spoken of as being exceptional.

One of them in particular had a horse that the Duke would love to possess himself. He had been at Eton with its owner, who would, of course, ride it.

"A steeplechase run by Watson is exactly what I want for my new horse," his friend had said. "Thank you a thousand times, Victor, for getting me asked to it. Who is this Lady Basset by the way? I do not seem to have heard of her."

"Nor had I until recently, Tom," the Duke replied, "but I believe that she has been living abroad and has an immense fortune left to her by her husband, who was killed shortly after their wedding."

"If he also left her fond of horses, one cannot ask for more," Tom commented, "and I only hope her cellar is as good as her stables!"

They had both laughed at this, but the Duke knew that he would enjoy the party even more if a number of his old friends were present at the same time.

And above all he would enjoy beating them in the steeplechase!

He reckoned that Lady Basset was arranging it all especially for him.

It did not surprise him or particularly worry him, as he had been pursued by women ever since he had left Eton and he was also well aware that in the Social world a Duke was placed very firmly at the top of the tree.

From that point one descended step by step in the marriage stakes until reaching a mere 'Honourable' at the bottom and after that there were only 'gentlemen' left to choose from.

The older his family, the more valuable a catch he was considered to be.

The Duke, whatever his family might say, had no intention of marrying just to produce an heir.

Of course he wanted sons – sons who would ride as well as he did and who would enjoy the country more than the town and who would be as anxious as he had been to travel the world.

Equally, he told himself, there was no hurry and the most disastrous action he could possibly take would be to marry someone who would soon bore him stiff, a woman he had no interests in common with.

He was always interested in anything new, whether it was a recently invented piece of machinery or a hitherto undiscovered mountain.

He found in consequence that the average woman's conversation, except when they told him how handsome and attractive he was, was not worth listening to.

"The trouble with you," one of his friends had said to him once, "is that everything has been too easy for you, Victor. If you were up against great difficulties, as most of us are because we do not have enough money, you would look on love in an entirely different way."

"I don't know what you mean," the Duke replied somewhat haughtily.

"Because you have all you could possibly want," his friend answered, "you have nothing to strive for, and that, I assure you, Victor, is *very* bad for you."

The Duke laughed.

"Why? In what particular way?"

"As you are growing older you are getting a little *blasé*," was the response. "And you don't have to fight for anything. Everything you desire, including women, falls into your arms like an overripe peach!"

The Duke had thrown a cushion at him and then they had wrestled together in a way that was in itself both amusing and boyish.

That the Duke had eventually won naturally went without saying and he demanded an apology.

"Alright," his friend gave in, "you win, Victor! I apologise! But one day, you mark my words, you will find yourself in a situation you cannot buy your way out of."

"I will let you know when it happens," the Duke promised him.

Having overcome his friend as he was determined to do, they drank a glass of champagne to commemorate his victory.

*

He was now walking back from the stables towards The Hall.

As he did so he wondered what had happened to the very beautiful girl he had seen the first day he arrived – there had been no sign of her since then.

She had certainly been incredibly lovely, or had he dreamt it?

Was it possible that this girl, who was so obviously a lady, yet was pretending to be lady's maid to his hostess, could be so extraordinarily exceptional that he had thought about her continually since their chance meeting?

'I must have imagined it,' he told himself. 'There is no likelihood of my seeing her again.'

He felt he could hardly ask his valet if she ate in the housekeeper's room.

Although he knew that his bedroom communicated with Lady Basset's, there had been no sign of the girl in the passage outside.

His valet had informed him with glee that he had managed to obtain a key for the communicating door and the Duke had accepted this without comment.

He had learned from considerable experience that it was a major mistake to have a communicating door in any bedroom where he stayed.

He reckoned that he was not mistaken when he had thought it ominous that Lady Basset was in the room next to his.

She was not as young or as sexually attractive as most of the women who pursued him in London.

He was fastidious, despite all his family said about the ladies with whom he had enjoyed *affaires-de-coeur*.

It was not only that he was afraid that the husband of the lady in question might protest, it was that he himself was looking for perfection.

He supposed all men like himself dreamt of finding an ideal woman – she would be beautiful, intelligent and would arouse in him sensations he had never yet felt.

Strangely enough he had wanted to be truly in love ever since he had read the great Classics.

He had adored his mother who had died when he was quite young and she held a place in his heart that no one else had ever filled. She had been so lovely, gentle, kind and understanding and he had felt when she died that somehow a part of him had gone with her.

His father had been broken-hearted and her death had made him somewhat resentful of those who were still alive while the woman he loved was no longer with him.

He had been harsh with his boys simply because he could not express in his own words that he understood they were feeling her loss as much as he was.

For the Duke, his darling mother, although he did not realise it, represented the love he was seeking.

Sometimes he felt he would never find love.

His father had often told him how he had first met his mother in a strange and unusual way – she was still in the schoolroom and from that moment he had never found any other woman so beautiful or so attractive.

When he married, he had been ten years older than his bride and yet he had known she had as much to teach him about life as he had to teach her about love.

They had been so blissfully happy – so happy that it had seemed so cruel, almost a crime, that she should have died of cancer just before her thirty-sixth birthday.

She had given him three children and he knew he had had a happiness that few men were privileged to enjoy in this world.

The whole County had mourned when the Duchess was taken to the churchyard and the flowers that seemed to cover the ground near her grave ranged from small bunches of wild flowers from village children to huge wreaths from the Royal Family.

"She was an angel from Heaven," one woman had sighed tearfully at the funeral to her eldest son.

The Duke had often thought that it was the truth and there would never be anyone like her, but he felt it was something he could not say to his family.

But he knew deep in his heart of hearts that until he found someone as wonderful and as lovely as his mother he would never marry.

Yet he was man enough to enjoy the company of

women if they were attractive and it was only sad that they were merely 'ships that passed in the night'.

Sooner rather than later he drifted away from them and slipped out of their hands and try as they might they were unable to entice him back.

Walking back from the stables the Duke passed the wrong turning to The Hall he had taken on the day of his arrival.

Instinctively he glanced down the path, wondering if he would again see the beautiful girl who had directed him to the front door.

'*Helsa*', he thought to himself.

No woman he had ever known had had that name and it certainly suited her.

He felt disappointed that, having seen her for that brief moment, he had never set eyes on her again.

Yet why should he?

After all, she was with the servants, whilst he was very much in the front of the house.

At the same time there was a definite mystery about her which he found intriguing and longed to solve.

Just why had she begged him so fervently not to mention he had seen her?

Why had she given him her right name and then corrected it quickly?

There had been a touch of fear in her voice and he had known by the look in her eyes that she was frightened.

Of whom or of what?

The questions kept coming into his mind.

Although he told himself he was being ridiculous, he found it quite impossible not to keep remembering how beautiful she was.

He wondered why she was hiding, if that was the right word for it, in The Hall.

It was certainly an impressive place – he had visited the picture gallery and he could understand that if indeed Lady Basset owned it, she must be understandably proud of such a unique collection.

There were pictures there which every collector of art in the country would be proud to possess and yet the Duke noticed that whenever he attempted to talk to Lady Basset about them, she kept changing the subject.

And she did not seem as knowledgeable about her gallery as she should be.

He had also realised that the French furniture in one of the reception rooms was exceptional and he expected it had been brought to England at the time of the Revolution.

Yet when he spoke about it to Lady Basset she did not seem to be at all interested – in fact she then turned the conversation round to what *he* possessed.

He had to admit that his own collections were not quite as outstanding as those he had seen in this house.

Lady Basset had told him she had been abroad and that was why a number of pictures needed cleaning and she had also said that there were parts of the house that really required restoring back to their original beauty.

"Surely there was someone here looking after the house while you were away?" the Duke had asked her.

Once again she wanted to talk about his house not hers.

"You must invite me to your house in London," she cooed. "I hear everything in it is fantastic, and, of course, most of all I would like to visit your house in the country."

"I think after what I have seen here you might be disappointed."

Lady Basset smiled.

"What I would like more than anything else would be to learn about what the Dukes of Mervinston have made theirs over many centuries. I am sure you have not only a wonderful library but a fantastic collection of china."

"I regret to say I don't think it is as good as your china in the drawing room. Do tell me how your ancestors acquired such a magnificent collection of Sèvres and also Chamberlain Worcester of which my father was so fond."

He remembered now that Lady Basset had avoided the questions by telling him about a collection she had seen in London. It had not seemed to him to be of any merit and yet she preferred to talk of that rather than what was on display just a few doors from where they were sitting.

The Duke wondered if she had any reason for being so elusive about her possessions and then he told himself it was probably just ignorance.

Though being hers she had not taken the interest in them that he would have done if they had belonged to him.

'At any rate,' he mused, 'I am not concerned with what Lady Basset thinks or does not think.'

*

What did concern him was the steeplechase.

He now had to wait another whole day before the promised race could take place.

Meanwhile he had been told that there was to be an early luncheon so they could start taking their horses over the jumps in the paddock as soon as it was finished.

As he reached the hall, the Duke was taken aback to see that Lady Basset was now moving towards him with her hands outstretched.

"I am terribly sorry, Your Grace," she purred, "that the steeplechase has had to be postponed. But we dare not take risks with someone like yourself."

She pressed his arm as she continued,

"But I can promise that you will find the jumps this afternoon challenging. Then this evening we have a local orchestra coming from the nearest town. So we can dance after dinner, which I am sure you will find amusing."

"You think of everything," the Duke observed.

There was little else he could say as Lady Basset slipped her arm through his.

"All I want to do," she said, "is to make your visit here happy and I feel sure I will find an easy way to do it."

She looked up into his eyes as she spoke.

He knew exactly what she was implying.

Equally at the back of his mind he wondered if it was really worthwhile staying until Monday.

CHAPTER FIVE

Helsa was determined to see the horses jumping.

But she thought it would be a mistake, especially as people from the village might be there, for her to go to the paddock.

She therefore walked to the West wing of The Hall where one of her many ancestors, who was apparently very eccentric in his ways, had added a Palladian tower.

From it he could look over the estate and see what everyone was doing. She had not been up the tower for years and the steps were very dusty, but when she reached the pinnacle it was exactly as it had always been.

There were windows all round it so that one could see for miles in every direction.

As a child she had discovered the skylight and she had been brave enough to climb through it onto the very top of the tower.

The skylight was still there and underneath it was a heavy wooden bed in which her ancestor had slept when he particularly wanted to know what was going on at night.

He had been 'a peeping Tom' in a big way and this was a continual joke in the family, Helsa recalled.

There was no need for her at the moment to climb up from the bed through the skylight onto the top of the roof as she could see the paddock very clearly from one of the windows and indeed every individual jump.

Gazing out she could see that the Duke was riding Masterpiece and she thought he looked more distinguished than anyone else in the paddock.

Lady Basset obviously thought the same as she was following him around and trying to attract his attention and even from this distance Helsa could see that he was much more interested in the jumps.

The others were mounting their horses and Watson was now giving orders for the jumping competition.

When it began, Helsa realised that each man had to go round the course three times and was timed by Watson.

He sent the Duke round first.

Helsa thought with a smile that he was challenging the other riders to beat what she was quite sure would be an almost unbeatable time.

Certainly Masterpiece deserved his name and she was sure that the Duke who seemed to go faster with each round would be impossible to equal let alone surpass.

She watched the other competitors and there were cheers when one gentleman on an exceptional horse, who was obviously an experienced jumper, tied with the Duke.

It was then that the two of them rode together for a deciding round.

While Helsa held her breath, the Duke won by just half a length.

By this time quite a crowd had gathered from the village and she was glad she had been sensible enough not to go into the paddock.

It was quite certain they would speak to her politely as 'Miss Helsa' and if Lady Basset heard them, she would undoubtedly be curious.

It was nearly teatime when the Duke won the final competition amid applause from all those present.

He raised his hand to acknowledge the cheers and, although Helsa could not hear what she was saying, Lady Basset appeared to be gushing at him.

She stood beside him patting his horse and looking up at him in a way that Helsa felt he must find somewhat embarrassing.

Then at last the Duke moved towards the stables followed by the rest of the riders.

They left their horses and walked into the house for tea.

Helsa climbed down from the tower and went to Lady Basset's bedroom as she was sure that her Ladyship would want to tidy herself before tea.

She was not mistaken as a few minutes later Lady Basset came bustling in through the bedroom door.

"His Grace won," she said, "as I was sure he would. I have a beautiful prize for him that I know he will enjoy."

"I thought that the prizes were in money," Helsa commented coyly.

"Yes, for the other riders, but as I was quite certain that the Duke would win, I was astute enough to provide a different prize that I know he will appreciate."

She spoke with satisfaction as if she could not keep the good news to herself.

Helsa poured out warm water for her to wash her hands and then she tidied her hair.

"After tea they are all going to a different sort of racing," Lady Basset remarked. "That should keep them happy. Personally I find horses such a bore, but gentlemen appear to enjoy them more than anything else."

There was a note in her voice that told Helsa she was thinking they should be concerning themselves with *her* and not with mere animals.

Helsa had, however, been wise enough since she had taken Mary's place to say as little as possible.

And having viewed the jumping competition Helsa thought it was unnecessary to climb the tower again.

Instead she decided to hurry back home to see if her father was alright as she was sure Lady Basset would not require her again until dinnertime.

So she walked slowly across the Park, enjoying its beauty with the sun streaming through the branches of the trees and the stags lying quietly beneath them.

However, when she reached the Vicarage she found her father was not there and Bessie had no idea when he would return.

She went to see Golden Arrow and when she was leaving, having made a fuss of him, she ran into George.

"What that there 'orse needs, Miss Helsa, be a bit of exercise," he said. "'E misses you takin' him out in the mornin' and if you leaves 'im too long, 'e'll get too fat to carry you!"

He was joking and Helsa laughed, but she realised that she must not neglect Golden Arrow.

"I'll surely come back and ride him early tomorrow morning," she promised. "So put him into his stall tonight, George, so that I need not waste time bringing him in from the field."

"I'll do that, Miss Helsa, and you can be sure 'e'll enjoy 'avin' you with 'im again."

Helsa smiled at him and then she retraced her steps back to The Hall.

She had heard that they were to dance tonight and she wondered how that was possible when apart from Lady Basset there were only the two elderly ladies for the nine gentlemen.

Then she learnt from Robinson that her Ladyship had heard of an orchestra in the nearest town, which not only played for people to dance but brought with them, if required, six girls who gave an exhibition of dancing.

"I hears that they dance as we would if we could," Robinson commented, "and then they gives the gentlemen as admires them a lesson, so to speak."

"How clever of Lady Basset to find anything quite so original here in the country!" exclaimed Helsa.

Robinson looked over his shoulder in case someone was listening and then he said in a whisper,

"I hears that she sent some of her staff down from London to find out what entertainment could be supplied here in the country. She were determined that the party should be kept amused if they had to stay longer than they expected."

Helsa stared at him.

"Why should she think, even before she had arrived here," she asked, "that they would have to stay longer than intended? After all the steeplechase was meant to be run today."

Robinson smiled.

Then once again he looked over his shoulder.

"If you asks me, Miss Helsa, she intended to keep the Duke here as long as she can!"

As he finished speaking, there came the sound of footsteps approaching and Helsa hurried away.

She now recognised that the postponement of the steeplechase had been in Lady Basset's mind from the very beginning.

Of course it would have been disappointing for her if the Duke had left first thing on Sunday morning, or even perhaps late this afternoon when the steeplechase ended.

Was the whole convoluted story about the fallen trees and Watson's worry over the course being dangerous simply fictitious?

Had it been a trick to keep the Duke at The Hall?

'She is certainly a very determined woman,' Helsa mused as she walked slowly upstairs.

Helsa felt sure the Duke would not be captivated by Lady Basset as she so wanted him to be – but she did not know exactly why she was so certain about this.

The Duke exuded an air of tenacity and pride which gave him, she recognised, his strong personality.

It would be difficult, she thought, to make him do anything he did not want to do and she knew too, almost instinctively, that he would not be attracted by someone like Lady Basset.

Her Ladyship, she admitted, was indeed appealing in her own way and she was also immensely rich.

But money did not concern the Duke as he was a very wealthy man.

Helsa had a feeling, although she could not express it to herself, that, as the Duke had an instinct for horses, he would undoubtedly possess the same instinct for people.

Lady Basset was not exceptional in any way, nor was she unusually alluring.

Helsa could not quite put it into words and yet ever since she had been small, she had learnt to assess people when she met them and to tell even before they spoke to her what they were like.

As her Papa would have said, she knew if they were 'good or bad'.

Lady Basset was obviously accustomed to getting her own way and this was probably due to her riches and yet her pursuit of the Duke had gone as far as deliberately postponing the running of the steeplechase.

Helsa wondered if the Duke had guessed what was going on and if he minded being stalked as if he was a wild animal by a woman determined to take him captive.

Then as she thought about it, she gave a little laugh.

Perhaps she was making a huge drama out of what was quite an ordinary everyday occurrence.

Women, whether they were young or old, always ran after a man who had a title and she could understand why, with all her possessions, Lady Basset wanted above all to be a Duchess.

At the same time Helsa wondered if any marriage which resulted from such dubious methods could ever be a happy one.

'When I marry,' she decided, 'I want to be in love just as Mama and Papa were. They fell in love with each other the first moment they met.'

It had not mattered to them whether they were rich or poor as long as they were both together. Naturally they would have liked more money and her father would have been overjoyed if he could have lived at The Hall after he had inherited.

Instead as their Vicar he had brought comfort and happiness to so many of the locals.

She felt that he had worked even harder since he had lost her wonderful mother, simply because he did not want to think about himself and his own suffering but of the needs of others.

'What they had was real love,' Helsa told herself. 'Papa now tries to give the love that he had for Mama to those who are lonely, unhappy and ill.'

*

She left a note for him on his desk to say she had come to see him and that she hoped he was not feeling too lonely.

She ended by saying how much she loved him and added to the note a long row of kisses. She left it on the blotter, so that he could not fail to see it when he went to his desk.

As she did so, she saw the long list of services that would take place tomorrow.

She had hoped that there would be a chance of her going to Matins if Lady Basset did not require her, but now she saw that Matins would take place in one of the other Parishes her father had to look after.

They did not have a Vicar of their own and for her Papa to apportion his time among three Parishes had been very difficult, but he managed to conduct one Service in each Church every Sunday.

Tomorrow, Helsa found, in their own Church they were having Evensong.

'I will find it difficult,' she thought, 'to go to that Service.'

From seven o'clock onwards she had to help Lady Basset change for dinner.

There was, however, a good chance she might see her father early in the morning when she came back to ride Golden Arrow, so she decided she would add a PS to her letter saying what she was intending to do.

Then she hurried back to The Hall.

On arrival she was to learn from Robinson that the orchestra had already arrived and they were in one of the rooms near the pantry where they were to change.

The dancers, Robinson told her, were already in the music room where the dancing was to take place.

There was a stately ballroom at The Hall, but it was very large and could in fact hold several hundred people.

The music room was quite small and very beautiful with a polished floor and a piano on a small platform.

"I do wish I could see them dance," she confided to Robinson without thinking.

"The girls are pretty enough to amuse all the young gentlemen here," Robinson replied. "But them who plays the music I can only hope make a better sound than they look!"

Helsa laughed as Robinson always had something funny to say about people.

"I would still like to see and to hear them. Perhaps I could at least listen to them in the room above the music room."

"That's a good idea, Miss Helsa. I'll open all the windows and you do the same in the room upstairs. And if nothing else, music travels on the air."

"That is true, and thank you very much, Robinson. I don't want to feel completely out of it."

"If you asks me," added Robinson, "you ought to be in it and having a ball here of your own. That's what you should have."

"You know as well as I do that we have not a penny to spare on such a frivolity as a ball."

"You'll have one one day, Miss Helsa, you mark my words – and it's what you deserves."

Helsa smiled at him and went upstairs.

She thought it would be so lovely if there really was to be a ball at The Hall for her, but there had not been enough money even to live quietly as they did, let alone think of balls or being presented at Court.

It was one of the privileges she was entitled to as her father's daughter.

'Maybe one day someone will wave a magic wand,' she reflected, 'and we will find a crock of gold at the end of the rainbow.'

At least there should be some benefits from Lady Basset renting The Hall, but Helsa knew any money that was spare her father would spend not on her but on the locals, who had been in want for so long and some of them were almost on the verge of starvation.

As she went upstairs she thought how magnificent The Hall looked with the afternoon sun shining on the many windows of the great house.

She wondered if it would ever be possible to live in it and it was one of her dreams that was *most* unlikely to ever come true.

Yet it would, she reckoned, make her father very happy, but he would not wish to live there unless he could help the villagers, which meant employing more men on the estate in the same way as they had been employed in the old days when his grandfather lived there.

Upstairs in Lady Basset's bedroom she laid out all the items her Ladyship would need when she changed for dinner.

She helped the maids to arrange the bath which her Ladyship always took in the evening. It meant the footmen carrying hot water up from the kitchen in brass cans and it took three maids to carry the bath into the bedroom.

They would set it down on the hearthrug in front of the fireplace and in the winter the fire warmed whoever was having a bath there.

But now because it was so warm the fireplace was filled with flowering plants.

It was Helsa who had told Cosnet that was what she wanted, when she begged him for flowers for every room.

Lady Basset came upstairs a little later than Helsa had expected her.

"I will have to hurry," she announced as she walked into the bedroom, "because I want to have a word with the dancers before they perform tonight and make it clear to them that they are expected to stay afterwards and dance with the gentlemen in the party."

"As there are only six of them, my Lady," Helsa came in, "the nine gentlemen who I understand are your guests will have to take turns."

Lady Basset laughed.

"Lord Miller and Sir James are too old to dance, but the other gentlemen are looking forward to it and naturally the Duke will be dancing with *me*."

She said the words with a note of triumph in her voice.

Then she looked at herself in the mirror as if to confirm that he would admire her as much as she admired herself.

Helsa said nothing.

She was wondering if any man especially the Duke, would really be attracted to a woman as bossy as Lady Basset.

However there was no doubt that she had organised the house magnificently and everything had gone smoothly so far without any unfortunate mishaps.

Helsa had to admit it was her Ladyship's hand on the wheel that had made everything go well, and yet there was a hard note in her voice when she was determined to have her own way and she could not help feeling that any man who was a man would resent it.

Lady Basset gave her orders almost like an Officer commanding troops who were not fully trained and had to be shouted at to make them understand what was required – there would be a stern frown on her forehead and her voice shuddered if everything was not exactly to her liking.

'She could run a school or a ship,' Helsa thought. 'But would any man, especially the Duke, want someone controlling, as it were, the very air he breathed?'

Then she told herself that she should be grateful to the Duke as all this display was very obviously an effort to please him and without that urgent desire of Lady Basset's, they would not be receiving a large rent for The Hall – and employing so many local people.

'I must be grateful, very grateful,' she told herself.

She wondered vaguely if finally Lady Basset would win and the Duke would succumb to her charms.

After dinner, when she heard the orchestra starting to play in the music room, she hurried up to the bedroom above.

She opened all the windows and, as she did so, she realised that Robinson had been true to his word and had opened the windows of the music room.

Now the music was very clear and seemed to merge into the darkness outside and then create a mystic aura that spread over the garden.

Helsa leaned on the windowsill, wishing she could see the dancers perform.

From the applause the audience gave at the end of one of the dances, she was quite certain that the girls had danced beautifully.

Lady Basset had indeed clocked up another winner!

Then the orchestra began to play a popular dance tune that Helsa instantly recognised and this meant that the young gentlemen would now be dancing with the dancers who had just performed.

Helsa was convinced that they would be enjoying themselves, as she leaned out of the window wishing again she could see what they were doing now.

Then one of the French windows which were on each side of the platform was opened.

To her surprise the Duke stepped out.

He stood for a moment looking at the garden and then he walked quickly over the lawn and disappeared into the shrubbery on the far side of it.

Helsa watched him until he was out of sight.

A moment later Lady Basset came out through the French window and stood gazing round her.

She was obviously searching for the Duke and as there was no sign of him, she walked a little further onto the lawn.

She stood there irresolute.

The moon was rising in the clear sky and the stars were coming out one by one.

In the shimmering light Lady Basset looked, Helsa thought, quite pretty and there was certainly no doubt that her evening gown, obviously a very expensive one, was exceedingly elegant.

As she stood there under the stars, she might have been a Goddess come down from Mount Olympus.

Yet romantic as she appeared in such surroundings she was alone and as far as Helsa could make out from the window there was still no sign of the Duke.

She felt that he had escaped deliberately and had no intention of returning until it suited him.

Almost as if her thoughts had been communicated to Lady Basset, she stamped her foot on the grass.

Then turning round, she walked briskly and rather aggressively back into the music room.

As she went Helsa thought that under her breath she was, if not swearing, then making sounds to herself which were very close to it.

Helsa listened to the music for some time and then she decided that she would be wise to retire to bed.

She had put everything ready for Lady Basset and had been told not to wait up for her and so she therefore felt free to go to her own room.

However, on the way there she paused to peep over the banisters on the first floor and saw that Robinson was still in the hall, giving the night-footman instructions as to the orchestra's requirements when they returned to their own rooms.

Then as he finished, he glanced up and saw Helsa.

"Be you going to bed, Miss Helsa?" he asked.

Helsa nodded.

"Thank you for opening the windows, Robinson. I loved listening to the music, but it has been a long day and I am a little tired."

"Not as tired as they'll all be when they turns in. I'd forgotten to inform you, Miss Helsa, that her Ladyship expects they'll be late and she don't want to be called until ten o'clock tomorrow morning."

"*Ten o'clock*! Oh, splendid! That means I can go home and ride Golden Arrow."

Helsa had forgotten for the moment that she was supposed to be Mary and as she finished speaking she gave a little murmur and put her fingers to her lips.

"It's all right," Robinson replied. "No one's heard you. If you do that, you'll be quite safe and if you asks me there'll be a lot of tired heads and feet tomorrow!"

Helsa laughed and then she went up the stairs to the nursery.

She climbed into her bed, but did not go to sleep for some time.

She was wondering, although it was no business of hers, whether the Duke had gone back to dance with Lady Basset – or perhaps he had been allowed to dance with one of the pretty dancers who had been hired for the evening.

When she finally fell asleep, she dreamed that she was riding the Duke's stallion, Masterpiece, and he was carrying her so effortlessly over the highest jumps that she felt she was flying through the air.

*

She had deliberately left the curtains undrawn over the windows and so the sun woke her just after six o'clock.

It was what she had hoped would happen.

She jumped swiftly out of her bed and put on her riding habit – she had brought it with her to The Hall just in case she was lucky enough to be able to sneak in a ride in between her duties.

Then she hurried downstairs.

The house was as quiet as a graveyard.

The night-footman was fast asleep in his padded chair in the hall.

She let herself out of the front door instead of going round the back and then ran through the Park disturbing the stags lying under the trees.

When she reached the Vicarage, she could see that her father's curtains were drawn back over his bedroom windows, and she felt sure that by this time he would have left to take Communion at one of his Parishes.

When she looked into the stables, she saw that his horse and cart had gone.

Golden Arrow was in his stall just as George had promised he would be and he was very pleased to see her and Helsa patted him and made a fuss of him before she put on his bridle and saddle.

He nuzzled against her and she sensed that he was as excited as she was at going for a ride.

They set off going through the garden into the Park and then on to the flat ground. She never wore a hat when she was riding on the estate as she so loved the feeling of the breeze in her hair.

Helsa gave Golden Arrow his head until they were out of sight of The Hall and then they reached the special wood on the estate that she loved more than all the others.

It was a wood of white elms that had been planted many years ago and Helsa believed that it was the most beautiful of all the woods on the estate.

She had no idea that, as she galloped over the fields towards it, that she had been seen by someone riding down from the stables.

He was following her at a distance, but keeping her in sight.

The Duke felt certain that her golden hair was the sign he was seeking, but would be impossible to ever find again.

He was following her, thinking that he had never in his life seen a woman ride better.

She had such an unmistakable elegance about her that she might have been one of the smart riders in Rotten Row, but even they could never compare with her prowess.

Then, as Helsa disappeared into a nearby wood, he increased his speed.

He was afraid she might vanish as she had done the first time he had encountered her.

Inside the wood Helsa was moving more slowly.

With the silvery leaves over her head and the moss beneath Golden Arrow's hooves, she felt that she was once again in a fairyland, which had been hers ever since she had been a child.

She believed that there were fairies in the garden and amongst the trees and bushes in the shrubbery, and she had at times been quite certain she had seen them twinkling in the sunshine.

Often she had told herself different stories as to what they were doing and why they were there.

It was her mother who had read to her first about fairies when she was very small, and on Sundays the fairy tales became religious and somehow she always connected them in her mind with angels.

They aroused in her what she felt when she saw the stars shining down at night onto the magical world below.

It was to the trees in the wood that she confided her troubles and all her difficulties and somehow, because they too were part of her fairyland, they always reassured her.

Everything would certainly work out right in the end, they would tell her – and she must not be frightened.

Now as she rode through the wood she was sending up a prayer of thankfulness that everything at The Hall had gone smoothly up to this moment.

Almost as if it was a gift from Heaven itself, Lady Basset had rented The Hall and it had made things so much easier for them financially.

'Thank you, thank you, God,' Helsa was saying in her heart.

She rode on to her favourite place in the centre of the wood. It was a little pool of sparkling water of which there were many in the woods.

But this was a particularly precious one.

She had been quite sure, when she had first been old enough to reach it from The Hall, that water nymphs lived there in the dark water and the kingcups and the irises growing round the pool were all part of the water nymphs themselves.

She pulled up Golden Arrow and bent her head to gaze into the water.

Then she suddenly became aware that a horse was approaching and she was not alone in the wood.

At first she was annoyed that anyone should disturb her.

And as the horse drew closer, she saw that the Duke was the rider.

She smiled as he approached her.

"I thought it must be you," he began, "when I saw your horse in the distance. But I had no idea you could ride so brilliantly."

"Allow me to introduce you to someone you have not met before, Your Grace. His name is Golden Arrow and although he is not as magnificent as your Masterpiece, I love him almost more than anyone else in the world."

The Duke grinned.

"How *could* anyone be so lucky or ask for more?"

Helsa turned towards the pool.

"This is a very special place, and let me tell Your Grace that you are very fortunate to be here."

"That is just what I was thinking myself," the Duke replied. "But tell me why it is so special."

"I come here if ever I am a little unhappy and the water nymphs talk to me and tell me everything will be all right in the end."

"Why should it ever be anything else where you are concerned, Helsa?"

She did not answer and after a moment the Duke enquired,

"Tell me what is troubling you, Helsa. I am good at answering puzzles and finding a way out of a maze."

"I guessed you would be like that, You Grace. At the same time I am sure you have enough troubles of your own without mine."

"I would like you to trust me – "

She turned to gaze at him.

"I am sure that a great number of people do trust you and that you never disappoint them. But unfortunately my problem is one I have to solve for myself. Therefore only the water nymphs will now listen to me and sometimes, although not always, they tell me what to do."

Helsa was talking as if in a dream, which somehow always seemed to come to her naturally whenever she was in this part of the wood.

She had no idea that the Duke was thinking that she was completely different from any woman he had ever met and almost too glorious to be real.

There was in fact something quite unreal about her that he could not put into words.

Then he dismounted and fixed Masterpiece's reins firmly to the saddle.

Without his saying anything, but almost as if he had given her an order, Helsa did the same and she knew that Golden Arrow would not move far away from her.

She left the horse and walked to where on one side of the clearing there was a pile of tree trunks that had been cut down a long time ago, but had been left piled on each other and they made an excellent seat as she had so often found before.

When she sat down, the Duke joined her.

"Do you come here very often?" he asked her.

"I have come here ever since I was old enough to ride alone. To me this is a place which has a magic I have never found anywhere else."

"I can guess that you have never been in love," the Duke remarked unexpectedly.

"Not in the way you mean," Helsa replied. "But I love a great number of people. My father, Golden Arrow and my mother, who died some time ago. But when I am here, she seems to be so close to me – "

She was speaking once again as if in a dream and it made the Duke realise that she was not thinking of him as a man, and he was probably someone who was to her a part of her enchanted wood and the many elves and goblins it undoubtedly housed.

He looked at her and was then aware that she was not looking at him but at the pool.

She was not just enchanting and ethereally beautiful but so very different from any of the other women he had spent so much of his time with – he had known so well from the brightness of their eyes and the movement of their lips that it was impossible for them to think of anyone or anything else but him.

But this strange and heavenly creature was not in the least bit concerned with him personally – only with the world beyond the world she was living in at the moment.

The Duke had travelled a great deal.

He thought that only in India, Nepal or Tibet had he found very few people who, while still of this world, were momentarily in their minds and souls in another.

There was silence for quite some minutes.

Then Helsa said,

"If you have anything at all that troubles you, ask the elves who are listening to us at this moment to help you, Your Grace. They have never failed me yet."

She gave a little sigh.

"I suppose we should be going back, but *please* do not tell anyone at The Hall where you have been."

"I know quite well that you would not want them running into this wood to see what you see. Not that they would see it, anyway."

"I knew you would understand, Your Grace."

"Why should you think that?"

"I don't know," she answered. "But the first time I saw you I thought there was something in your voice and your eyes that made you stand out from the others.

"I do think, Your Grace, you are seeking something that you have not yet found – something that always eludes you, although you cannot think why it should."

The Duke was still.

He was listening, but he did not speak.

"Something tells me," Helsa went on, "that you will always win, though sometimes it will be difficult. But you must never give up."

The Duke was too surprised to make any reply.

Almost as if she had forgotten his very existence, Helsa then rose from the woodpile and walked to her horse.

It was only as she actually reached Golden Arrow that the Duke joined her.

Picking her up, he lifted her onto the saddle.

She took up the reins and turned towards the path that led out of the wood.

She did not speak nor did she seem to be waiting for him.

The Duke mounted Masterpiece and followed her.

Only when they were out of the wood itself did he draw up beside Helsa.

"Where are you going now?" he asked her gently.

"I shall take Golden Arrow home and then I will come back to The Hall. It is nearly time for breakfast and *please* don't tell anyone you have seen me."

"I promise I will not do so," affirmed the Duke.

She gave him a little smile and then rode away.

He stood for a few moments watching her until she disappeared under the trees into the Park.

Then slowly he rode back to the stables at The Hall.

He was thinking that it was the strangest morning he had ever spent.

Helsa was so totally unlike any woman he had ever encountered.

CHAPTER SIX

As Monday morning arrived, Helsa could feel the excitement vibrating through the house.

At last they were to run the steeplechase.

Everyone felt that if they hurried they would speed up the moment for it to start.

When her breakfast was brought upstairs, it was put swiftly down on the table and the footman vanished before she could say 'thank you'.

Like all the other young men in the house, he was determined to be in the paddock when Watson started the race.

As Lady Basset was to be there as well, Helsa had made her own plans.

She was thankful that by the time the guests in the house had left for the stables or the paddock, she had not been given another duty.

Fortunately she knew a better place to see it from than they did.

The maids were busy tidying Lady Basset's room and all Helsa had to do was to put away the jewellery her Ladyship had worn the night before.

Then she ran along the passage to the West wing.

Everything was silent as everyone was either riding in or watching the steeplechase.

She climbed up to the top floor and then again up the smaller steps that led to the tower –

She could see the start clearly from the windows of the tower, but today she was determined to go right up to the roof.

She knew that from there she would have a better view than from anywhere on the ground.

She climbed, as she had so often as a child, onto the firm end of the old bed and reached up towards the skylight.

She pushed it open and was relieved that it had not become solid over the years and then squeezed herself out onto the roof of the tower.

No one could have a better view than from here and she thought that she could actually see the boundary of the estate in the distance.

She could see all the woods the riders would pass through. In some of them there were steep stony paths on which they would have to tread more slowly and carefully than anywhere else.

There was no need for Helsa to stand and anyway she might have been seen. So she sat down and she could then see everyone in the paddock quite clearly through the bars of the parapet.

Lady Basset was there and it was no surprise that she was talking eagerly to the Duke, who was mounted on Masterpiece.

Helsa could not help but wonder if poor Samson, who had been left behind, realised what he was missing.

The young gentlemen staying in the house were all mounted on their own horses and she was forced to admit that they were all outstanding animals.

Watson was getting them all into line and telling them – what they already knew – exactly the route they had to take.

Actually the course had all been clearly marked out with coloured ribbons and from what Helsa had overheard, it would be almost impossible for anyone to go wrong.

It was a very long course, the longest she thought, that had ever been held on the Irvin estate.

Then Watson turned to the riders, gave the starting signal and *they were off*.

The great steeplechase had at last begun and there were more than twenty horses participating in the race.

The Duke was looking resplendent in his bright red jacket and black top hat and Helsa thought that the horses brought by the neighbours had a poor chance of finishing the course.

She watched them intently as they galloped across the first field – and then the second.

The Duke was already well out in front, but Helsa could see that he was pulling in Masterpiece and not letting him tire himself out too soon.

She could observe from her outstanding view that Watson had made the course a very hard one and she was more than ever convinced that only half the competitors would finish the race.

She saw Lady Basset, having seen the start of the race, hurry across the paddock and into the house. One or two people attempted to speak to her, but she waved them on one side.

Helsa wondered why she was in such a hurry.

She hoped it was not because she thought she might watch the steeplechase from the tower too and even so she was not likely to climb up onto the roof – and because she was larger than her, she would never be able squeeze her body through the skylight.

So Helsa concentrated on the steeplechase.

She was trying to see, although it was sometimes difficult, if the Duke was still in front of the other riders.

'I do want Masterpiece to win,' she thought. 'If it was not for the Duke, the steeplechase would not be taking place at all.'

She only wished her father could watch it too, but she was sure he would be busy in one of his three Parishes.

'I will tell him about it afterwards,' she promised herself.

Then suddenly to her surprise she heard the door into the room below open.

"Your Ladyship will see perfectly well from 'ere," she heard a man's rough voice saying.

Helsa tensed.

It was obvious that Lady Basset had been brought up here to the tower by someone whose voice she did not recognise to enjoy a really good view of the steeplechase.

It was fortunate, Helsa now reflected, that she had climbed onto the roof and it was most unlikely they would have the slightest idea that she was there.

"Now show me exactly where I have to go," Lady Basset was asking.

"It's quite simple," the man answered. "I can show you from 'ere that you can ride out from the front of the 'ouse and through yon orchard and into the field beyond."

"Yes, yes, I can see that quite clearly," Lady Basset responded in a somewhat agitated way

"Avoid them trees on the left 'and side," the man went on, "then ride perfectly straight for about 'alf a mile before you reach the wood I am pointin' out now."

"Yes, yes," Lady Basset murmured. "I can see it rising up at the end."

"Exactly," he added. "That is where the men are 'iding who are waitin' for you."

Helsa did not understand what was going on.

"You are certain I will not be seen?" Lady Basset asked her mysterious companion.

"Does it matter if your Ladyship is seen?" the man questioned. "After all, you want to be at the end of the steeplechase and that is the point where they turn and ride back as quickly as they can to the winnin' post."

"Yes, yes, now I understand – but have I time?"

The man gave a laugh and it was not a particularly pleasant sound.

"Plenty of time, my Lady. Watson assured me it would take them an hour and a 'alf to reach that point and by the time they get there your 'orse will be out of sight and you will be bound up and in the slate mine."

Listening, Helsa thought she must be dreaming.

Or else imagining in some strange way all she was overhearing.

"Yes, that is what Watson told me," Lady Basset remarked. "I hope they will be gentle with me."

"Of course they will. It'll only be 'is Grace who is likely to put up a fight. They will just take you into the mine and then bring 'is Grace the Duke down and set 'im beside you."

Overhead Helsa gave a little gasp.

But she dare not move in case they realised she was there.

"Now this is the most difficult bit," the man below was saying.

"Go over with me once again exactly what is going to happen, Tybolt, so that there will be no mistakes," Lady Basset demanded.

"Well, as soon as your Ladyship and 'is Grace are tied up and findin' it impossible to move, I'll then come in. When you see me you'll exclaim, '*Silas*!' as though I was the last person on earth you expected."

"Then what do you say?"

"I reply, 'this is my revenge and I'm goin' to leave you both 'ere till you die of starvation!' You must give a scream and plead with me."

"What do I say?" Lady Basset asked him.

"You beg me to forgive you if you 'urt me when you refused to marry me, sayin' you only wanted to marry the man you love."

There was a pause as if the man called Tybolt was thinking and then he added,

"I will say, 'well, now you can die with the man you love and I just 'ope that'll make you 'appy!' Then you start to cry. The Duke will probably say somethin' and if he does I'll answer 'im, but 'e'll be roped so that he cannot move."

"You'll make certain of that, Tybolt?"

"Sure I will. Now this is the trickiest bit."

Helsa was listening intently and Lady Basset was obviously listening too.

After a moment's silence Tybolt continued,

"You must cough as if it's too difficult for you to speak. Then you must gasp and splutter, 'the dust from the slate is makin' it difficult for me to breathe.' It is then I draw a bottle from my pocket."

"*A bottle*?"

"Because I am an 'umane man I say," Tybolt went on. "I'm goin' to give you somethin' to ease your throat and if I'm 'onest I don't want you to die too quickly."

"You must say, 'you are a cruel wicked man,' and then cough again. 'Take a drink of this,' I'll say, puttin' the bottle to your lips. But be sure you don't swallow any of it."

"I think I understand," murmured Lady Basset.

"Then I'll turn to the Duke and say, 'I suppose if I'm charitable to 'er who has 'urt me so much, I should be charitable to you too'. I'll 'old the bottle up to his lips and you must cough at the same time just in case 'e makes any effort not to accept it."

"Then you will force the drink down his throat?" Lady Basset asked.

"If 'e swallows too much of what's in that bottle, 'e'll be unable to speak, but it's essential he should be able to."

"Yes, of course. I understand that he will have just enough so that his brain is not functioning properly, but he will do as the Priest tells him."

"He will then repeat every word 'e is told," Tybolt replied with glee.

"You are sure of that, Tybolt?"

"As sure as I'm standin' 'ere."

"And the Priest? Where will he be while all this is going on?" Lady Basset enquired sharply.

"'E'll be 'iding outside the mine. 'E'll come in the moment I signal to 'im, which will be as soon as the drug works on the Duke."

"*Then he will marry us*," Lady Basset cried eagerly.

"'E'll marry you and I'll be a witness that 'e did so and so will a man who 'as come down from London with the Priest."

"I see that you have arranged everything perfectly, Tybolt, just as I wanted you to," sighed Lady Basset.

"I have carried out your orders, my Lady, and I'll be grateful if I can 'ave the money you promised me now."

"It is here," said Lady Basset, "and be careful you don't lose it."

There was silence while Helsa presumed that she was passing a package over to him.

Then Helsa heard her ask in a very different tone,

"You are sure he really is a Priest."

"I promise you I have checked 'im thoroughly and 'e is the incumbent at a Church in the East End. But 'e's fallen on 'ard times and like everyone else 'e needs the cash."

"We are certainly paying him most generously," commented Lady Basset sourly.

"To get the best you 'ave to pay the best," Tybolt retorted. "Now, my Lady, you should be on your way. The 'orse is waitin' for you at the front door and I told the groom you wished to ride alone and not be accompanied."

"Quite right," grunted Lady Basset.

"Now look once again to where you are goin'," he urged her, pointing where he had pointed earlier. "And there's no 'urry, you 'ave plenty of time. But the sooner you're in that slate mine the better."

"I am leaving at once," Lady Basset insisted, "and thank you very much for your help. You will not fail to rescue us on time?"

"No, of course not. As soon as the Priest has left we must give the Duke a little time to recover from the drug, although he will doubtless suffer a severe 'eadache for the rest of the day. Then we will come in and set both of you free."

"Thank you again, Tybolt, I will leave as soon as I go downstairs."

Helsa heard her leave the room and descending the narrow staircase.

She did not move, but held her breath until she heard the man called Tybolt follow her.

Even then she waited for what seemed an eternity of time until she dared slip down through the skylight onto the old bed.

She opened the door of the tower very cautiously, just in case Tybolt was still hanging about.

But there was no one to be seen.

Helsa hurried out of the West wing and towards the back of the house.

There appeared to be no one about and she was sure that the footmen and even Mr. Martin were still outside seeing what they could of the steeplechase.

She ran as fast as she could the quickest way to the stables.

When she got there, she found, as she had expected, that every stall was empty except for Samson's.

He was looking, she felt, somewhat forlorn at being left behind.

Because she had always looked after Golden Arrow herself, it was no trouble to saddle and bridle Samson.

She then rode out of the stable yard without anyone realising that she had been there.

She knew the country well and had ridden in every field and wood in which the steeplechase was now taking place.

She therefore knew exactly where the horses would be forced to slow down to walking pace.

And she would be able to warn the Duke what was waiting for him at the top of Monk Wood.

She had not visited the slate mine for years, but she knew exactly where it was – in Monk Wood.

Her father had taken her into it when she had been about nine years old and he had told her how at one time, when slate had been in demand, it had been busy with men cutting it out of the rock face.

Samson was delighted to be free.

As she could feel that he wanted to gallop, Helsa let him do so until they were out of sight of The Hall.

Then she felt safer and realising that she had plenty of time, she made him go slower.

The problem that now presented itself to her was that the Duke might not believe her incredibly far-fetched story.

Worse still, he might not be far enough ahead of the other riders and then it would be very hard for her to stop him.

There was a place at the very foot of Monk Wood where she knew it would be impossible for any rider to hurry and the path that led upwards was steep and rough – at the same time it was an excellent test in a steeplechase for those who believed it could easily be won in a gallop.

'That is where I must stop the Duke,' she decided and once again she was afraid that he might refuse to do so or to listen to her.

Because she was so nervous it seemed as if the way towards Monk Wood was far further than it really was.

In fact Helsa was almost afraid that the Duke would have ridden past and gone unsuspecting to his doom.

It seemed to her absolutely incredible that such an astonishing plot could have been devised by Lady Basset, so that she could get her own way and become the Duke's wife by deceit and subterfuge.

Equally Helsa had to admit that her plan had been well thought out and with a diabolical cleverness that made her shiver because it was so evil.

'How could any woman,' she reflected, 'demean herself to trap and capture a man and to force him into matrimony *just because he is a Duke*?'

She knew how horrified her father would be.

Yet if the Duke was married by a legitimate Priest and there were witnesses to the marriage, there could be no doubt it had actually taken place.

And it would be impossible for the Duke to free himself without the scandal of a divorce – a divorce which would have to go through an Act of Parliament and take years to finalise.

It was the wickedest plot ever thought up against a man who had done Lady Basset no harm – except of course to refuse her obvious advances because she did not attract him.

'I must save him, I *must*,' Helsa determined.

She was frightened once again that he would ride past her refusing to listen to her pleas and believe such an extraordinary and unlikely story.

At last, and it seemed to her to take a century, she reached the bottom of Monk Wood and it was where it joined another wood.

The steep climb to the top of it began here and she could see that Watson had put red ribbons all the way up it.

It would be impossible for two competitors in this steeplechase to ride up it side by side and that at least, she thought, was one point in her favour.

She pulled in Samson and then stood looking at the incline.

It was then that she decided it would be easier to tell the Duke what was happening if she was not mounted.

So she slipped down from Samson's back and tied his reins to a fallen tree.

Then she walked over the stones and dead leaves to the beribboned ascent and climbed until she was just far enough up to be out of sight of anyone approaching.

Helsa waited.

She could not make out any sound of horses in the distance – there was only the chirping of little birds and the rustle of rabbits in the undergrowth.

Yet she knew, lurking at the top of the wood, there were four men determined to take the Duke prisoner and to force him into the slate mine where Lady Basset would by now be waiting for him.

Her father had taught her to pray when she was a small child and frightened by thunderstorms.

After that she prayed when she was afraid of the dark or of ghosts she thought lurked in some parts of The Hall. She had known then that God and his angels would protect her.

She now prayed frantically and fervently not for herself but for the Duke.

How could the Duke suspect for one moment that any woman he met in the Social world could ever behave in such a cruel and wanton manner?

He would find it impossible to believe that anyone could desire his title so desperately that she would go to such extremes.

'I must save him, I must!' Helsa prayed. 'Please God help me! Please make him listen to me. *Please make him believe me.*'

She repeated the words over and over again.

Suddenly she heard a horse approaching.

It was travelling quite quickly.

She knew that was because the path through the wood where she was now standing was mossy – she had often ridden through it on Golden Arrow.

She, however, always stopped when she reached the climb to Monk Wood as she knew it was so dangerous.

The sound of hooves was growing louder.

She drew in her breath afraid that it might not be the Duke – or, if it was him, that he would be angry at finding her blocking his way.

She pressed her fingers together until they almost hurt and then, as she saw him riding not too fast towards her, she realised that the moment had come.

The Duke was looking down as if to see what the ground in front of him was like.

For a moment he did not see her.

Then he suddenly looked up and saw Helsa.

For just a moment he was only aware that she was unbelievably lovely.

He thought that as she was not in riding clothes she must have walked there.

Then, as he looked at her with a smile, he saw that she was holding up her hand as if to stop him.

He was well in front of the other competitors and there was only perhaps another half a mile to go before he would win the steeplechase.

At the same time it was always a mistake to stop when one was so far ahead.

As he approached Helsa, he expected her to get out of his way, but she remained stationless in front of him.

Without the Duke pulling at his reins Masterpiece recognised that he could not go any further.

Helsa ran to his side.

"*What is it?* Why are you stopping me?" the Duke demanded.

"You cannot go any further," cried Helsa. "There are men at the top of this wood waiting to force you off your horse and pull you into the slate mine."

"What are you talking about?" the Duke enquired. "I don't understand."

"Lady Basset is waiting there with a Priest *who will marry you!*"

The Duke stared at her.

"Is this a joke?"

"No, it is true and you have to believe me, Your Grace. I swear to you on everything I hold sacred that this is a plot against you. Lady Basset has a genuine Priest there who she has bribed to take the Service. They will first drug you with a liquid, which they will force you to drink, so that you do not know what you are doing."

The Duke looked at her in bewilderment.

"I find this – very hard to believe," he stammered.

"Of course you do, Your Grace, but I swear what I have told you is the truth and the complete truth."

Helsa drew in her breath before continuing,

"If you proceed any further you will find yourself married to Lady Basset, because they have a drug that will prevent your brain from working, although you will make the right responses and there are two men who will witness that you are actually married to her."

The Duke was silent for a moment and then he said,

"I suppose I have to believe you, although it seems to me just incredible and such a tale could only come from some adventure story and not real life."

"It is all true, Your Grace, I swear to you it is. So *please*, please ride back to The Hall and, if you are wise, you will leave immediately for London."

She reckoned that as the Priest would still be there, Lady Basset might find some other way of tricking him into matrimony.

The Duke was silent and still hesitating.

Helsa looked past him and down the path on which she had just come.

As if she had asked the question, the Duke added rather petulantly,

"I am well ahead of the field and I am very anxious for Masterpiece to win the steeplechase."

"I know! I know!" cried Helsa, "but he will not win – they will merely think you had a fall and the others will ride past without realising you are held a captive in the slate mine."

The Duke sighed.

"Well, I suppose I must accept that you are telling me the truth and I must be grateful you are saving me."

"How could you possibly marry any woman, Your Grace, who would contrive in such a cruel and wicked way to force you into it against your will?"

The Duke still looked rather indecisive before he finally turned to Helsa again,

"Now tell me what I must do?" the Duke asked. "Otherwise we could be joined by young Ashley who is riding, in my opinion, the only horse capable of competing with Masterpiece."

"Follow me," Helsa said quickly. "I will show you a route where no one will see you. I think you will have to admit at the stables you thought Masterpiece was limping a little and so you were forced to withdraw from the race."

The Duke smiled at her as if he thought it was very intelligent of her to have worked it all out.

But he did not say anything.

Helsa then walked ahead of him to where she had tied up Samson.

The Duke looked in amazement at his other horse.

"So you came on Samson?"

"When I heard what was happening, Your Grace, I ran to the stables as quickly as I could. He was the only horse left there."

"I am sure he is delighted you should ride him!"

"He is wonderful and we reached here in double quick time."

Helsa pointed to the other side of the wood,

"Go down there for about a mile and you will meet no one, because they are all out on the course watching the steeplechase. Then you can go straight back to The Hall."

"Where will you be going?" the Duke asked her.

"I will take Samson back through the wood where we met yesterday and merely say I was exercising him. No one will think it strange, even though I am not dressed for riding."

The Duke was reflecting that despite Helsa's full skirt, she managed to mount Samson most gracefully and she looked exquisitely lovely on the great horse.

"I think I can hear people in the distance. Hurry now, Your Grace, until you are behind rather than in front of them. Then you will be safe."

"I will do so, Helsa, although I still think this is part of a dream and not really taking place."

"That is what I felt myself when I overheard what they intended to do. I was only frightened you would not listen to me."

"I think that I will always listen to you, Helsa, and thank you so much for protecting me."

He smiled at her as he rode off.

Samson wanted to follow, but she held him back.

Helsa waited until she heard the other competitors riding through Monk Wood.

Then slowly, in the opposite direction to the way the Duke had gone, she rode back towards The Hall.

She rode through the wood she loved so much, but did not stop.

She reached the stables just as the winner of the steeplechase was riding at top speed towards the winning post.

It had taken her some time as she had not hurried and she was praying in her heart that the Duke had done exactly as she had told him.

No one would believe that he would pull out of the steeplechase when he so far ahead unless he had thought it seriously damaging to his precious stallion.

As she rode into the yard, one of the grooms came out to meet her.

"I thinks per'aps Samson 'ad escaped, Miss Helsa, when no one be 'ere," the man was complaining.

"I took him for a ride because he looked so lonely," she replied. "Have you heard who won the steeplechase?"

"I can tell you, Miss Helsa, who ain't won it and that be 'is Grace. 'E comes in 'ere a short time ago and says that fine stallion of 'is 'as sprained 'is leg. 'E told 'is groom to take 'im back to 'is own stables at once. Then 'e orders 'is chaise and drives orf!"

Helsa gave a deep sigh of relief.

The Duke had obeyed her and gone away just as she had advised him to do and he had not waited to say goodbye to Lady Basset.

She would doubtless be furious that he had decided not to finish the race and so avoided being captured by her gang of ruffians.

And therefore all her Ladyship's dastardly plotting and scheming had come to nothing.

Now massive cheers and shouts were coming from the direction of the paddock.

Helsa then knew that by now someone had won the steeplechase and the house party would be coming back to The Hall, but it would, however, still take them some time because there were prizes to be given out first.

She supposed Lady Basset would have deputised Watson to do the honours for her.

'I had better go into the house,' she thought, 'and make sure that everything is alright. Then I will wait for Lady Basset's fury when she finds out that the Duke has gone back to London.'

*

It then suddenly struck Helsa that she herself would never see him again and the thought brought tears to her eyes.

It had been so exciting meeting the Duke –

To talk to him in her very special magical wood.

To know that almost in spite of himself he believed her when she had told him that he was in great danger.

He had moved even quicker than she had expected and she could well understand that he had no wish to see Lady Basset.

Or, in fact, to have anything to do with the party which might have proved so disastrous for him personally.

Having patted Samson, Helsa then walked slowly towards The Hall.

There were still cheers and clapping of hands to be heard in the paddock and that meant the last competitors were passing the winning post.

Even if they did not win they were to be given a small souvenir with which to remember the steeplechase.

It was her grandfather who had introduced the idea and in his day there had been a steeplechase at The Hall every year and the villagers still talked about it.

Helsa knew it was unlikely that Lady Basset would stay in The Hall for long and so she went straight upstairs to the nursery.

There had been no sign of Robinson in the hall and she wondered if he had been there when the Duke returned and had assisted him in leaving as quickly as he could.

It would not have taken very long to have made the chaise ready and it was unlikely that the Duke would have changed from his red coat.

He would therefore have merely had to collect his valet and his luggage and Helsa could not help thinking that his valet might be used to receiving unexpected orders and so would not have taken long to pack.

In fact the Duke might have been intending in any case to leave immediately after the steeplechase.

She had a feeling when she had seen him disappear last night into the garden that he was thinking 'enough is enough' and might have decided then to return to London as soon as he possibly could.

'So I will never see him again,' Helsa sighed to herself.

She took the last step up the narrow stairs that led to the nursery and as she opened the nursery door, she gave a little cry of astonishment.

Sitting by the window was none other than Mary Emerson.

"Mary!" exclaimed Helsa. "You are back already!"

"Yes, I am back," answered Mary. "Grandmama was buried this morning and I thought the sooner I came here to help you the better."

"Dear Mary! I have indeed managed reasonably well without you, but I am so delighted to see you again."

"I thought you would be, Helsa. Now you can go back to the Vicarage and look after your dear father, which I know has been worrying you. But I could not come any sooner."

"No, of course not. I am very sorry to hear about your grandmother, Mary."

"It was a merciful death, as it happened. She was very old and had been in pain for a long time. The doctor could really do nothing for her."

Then, as if Mary wished to change the subject, she remarked,

"I can see you have been busy today. I thought the steeplechase was to be held on Saturday."

"Yes, it was, but it had to be postponed until today and I wish you had been able to see the outstanding horses that took part in it."

"Do you know who won?" enquired Mary.

"No, not yet. I have just come from the stables, but they were still cheering in the paddock, so obviously they have not finished giving away the prizes."

"You must tell me who is in the party," said Mary, "and if Lady Basset is very difficult to look after."

"Actually she is not as difficult as one might have expected, but I would be very grateful, dear Mary, if you could take over from me now. She had been plotting and planning the steeplechase and a great many other things, so I really have no wish to cope with her at the moment."

Mary smiled.

"Then I will do it for you. I am extremely grateful that you are not angry with me for having to let you down at the very last moment, Helsa."

"It has been a great help to Papa that Lady Basset rented The Hall and I hope we have made some money out of it. But I have a feeling that now the steeplechase is over she will rapidly return to London."

"I expect she finds the country rather dull and it's not surprising. With her money she could be going round the world and that is something I would surely like to do myself one day."

Helsa smiled at her.

"So would I, Mary, but now you are here I will go home to see Papa. I promise you to come back later today or tomorrow and see what is happening."

Helsa had gone into the night nursery to pack the few clothes she had brought with her. She had taken her case from the wardrobe and now she was filling it.

"I suppose her Ladyship is in the master bedroom," Mary asked her casually.

"No, she is in the room next door."

"Then who is in there?" Mary wanted to know.

"The Duke of Mervinston. I suppose you are aware that Dukes are always given the best of everything just because they are Dukes!"

Mary laughed.

"That is nice for them, but a bit disappointing for everyone else. Did you meet him?"

"Yes, I did – "

Helsa was putting one of her gowns carefully into the case and she tried to speak as if her meeting with the Duke had been of no consequence.

"Well, you were obviously not impressed," Mary added. "I had hoped at least one of the party would be attractive and someone we could then talk about afterwards even if they were not interested in us."

"How could you expect them to be interested when we are pretending to be servants?" Helsa pointed out.

Mary shrugged her shoulders.

"I have always believed that social standing would not be important if one met the right man – "

There was silence for a moment.

Then Helsa commented,

"Yes, of course, that is the right way to put it. If one met the right man, it would not matter."

"Well, there is always tomorrow," Mary remarked cheerfully. "Quite frankly it is about time both you and I found young men to admire us even in this dismal part of the world where nothing seems to happen."

"Except a steeplechase – " murmured Helsa.

She then closed the case knowing that she had put in everything she had brought.

"It is angelic of you to come so quickly, Mary, and now I must go home and see if Papa is well."

"Of course, Helsa, please don't worry. I will cope with everything here. It will cheer me up after seeing my relations and having to attend the funeral."

Helsa kissed her.

"I am more grateful than I can possibly say, Mary."

Carrying her case she walked out of the nursery and down the stairs.

As she reached the first floor, she heard the riders coming in through the front door, laughing and talking and they had obviously enjoyed themselves thoroughly.

Helsa then turned towards one of the side doors and slipped out of the house into the garden.

She walked along behind the rhododendrons until she reached the orchard and from there she found her way into the Park.

She had seen no one and no one had seen her.

She walked on, finding that her suitcase was not too heavy but a bother to carry.

Helsa could not help but think that she was going back to the old routine of no one to see or talk to except her father, who, when he came home late in the evening, was often too tired to even discuss anything with her.

It had been a great adventure meeting the Duke, but she was resigned that she would never see him again.

She had at least saved him from the wicked plotting and scheming of Lady Basset.

But just as her Ladyship had lost him, she had lost him too.

Helsa walked on doggedly towards the Vicarage for once taking no notice of the stags or the beauty of the Park.

Quite suddenly she knew that she loved the Duke with all her heart and soul.

CHAPTER SEVEN

Helsa reached the door in the wall that led into the Vicarage garden.

She walked through it, being careful not to bang her case against the sides and closed the door behind her.

The garden was full of delightful blooms and they did not seem to have suffered at all from her neglect these last few days when she had been at The Hall.

She walked across the lawn and putting down her case she went straight into the stables.

She thought if her father was back home his horse would be there, but the stalls were empty and quite clearly Golden Arrow was in the field and her father still away.

There was no sign of George the groom anywhere and she guessed he would have been watching the climax of the steeplechase.

She retraced her steps to the front of the Vicarage and picked up her case.

The front door was open because, as they were so loved in the village, both she and her father knew that no one would ever burgle them.

Instead of climbing up the stairs as she ordinarily would have done to unpack, Helsa went towards the study.

She somehow wanted to wait there for her father to return and to feel that, when he was with her, life would soon be back to normal.

There would be no need for her to go on thinking about the Duke and remembering his handsome face.

She realised it would be very difficult, now she was aware of her true feelings for him, to think of anything else.

But she told herself that this chapter of her life had closed and she must turn for consolation to her books that had meant so much to her these past years.

She opened the study door and walked in.

As she did so she looked towards the bookshelves that lined the wall behind her father's desk.

There was a sudden movement from the fireplace as she passed it.

She turned round and was frozen into immobility.

Rising from the chair where he had been sitting and reading a newspaper was *the Duke*.

For a second she thought he must be an illusion and that she was imagining he was there.

Then, as he threw the newspaper onto the floor, she stammered,

"It is *you* – but I thought – you had gone – "

She tripped over the words because it was almost impossible to speak.

The Duke smiled at her.

"Did you really think that after you have saved me from a fate worse than death, I would leave without saying goodbye and thank you?"

"But – your horses had gone from the stables – "

"They were waiting for me a little further up the road."

"But – how did you know – *who* I was?"

"It was not difficult to ask where a very beautiful young girl called Helsa lived and who was the owner of a horse called Golden Arrow!"

"So – you came – here," Helsa murmured.

"I came to find you, Helsa, and I knew you would come here sooner or later."

He moved closer to her as he spoke.

And now he stood looking down at her.

"How could you, looking as lovely as you do," he asked almost as if he was talking to himself, "be so clever and brave to save me from an awful fate I cannot really bear to think about?"

"You must forget it, Your Grace, and that will be easy when you go back to London – and are with your own friends – ?"

Then she suddenly gave a little cry.

"You don't think – that Lady Basset will try to trap you – again?"

"She may do, but it is not very likely, unless you save me again."

"How could I possibly save you – when you are in London? And it would be even more dangerous if you stay here."

"I know that," said the Duke, "but I have a solution to my problem."

"What is it?" Helsa implored him, "and will it keep you – really safe?"

"It will keep me really safe, but before I talk about that, I want to thank you for being so courageous in saving me. And, what I reckon was even more difficult, to make me believe you when you told me exactly what was going to happen."

"I was so frightened you would think I was lying or had been misled, Your Grace. In fact I prayed and prayed all the time I was waiting for you – that you would believe me."

"I did believe you, Helsa, and I knew for certain when I rode back to the paddock and saw Watson's look of astonishment on his face that you had told me the truth."

"*He was in on the plot too*? – and that was why he arranged for us to have the steeplechase today instead of on Saturday."

"So that it gave Lady Basset more time to be with me," the Duke added quietly.

"Exactly!" Helsa agreed, "but I think they had had some difficulty in finding a real Priest to marry you."

There was a pause and then the Duke muttered,

"I was wise enough to believe you, Helsa, and now I must try to thank you properly for saving me. I feel that words are impossible and there is only one way to do it."

He put his arms round Helsa as he spoke and drew her close to him.

Almost before she could breathe in or realise what was happening his lips were on hers.

He kissed her very gently.

Then, as he felt a tremor run through her, his arms held her closer.

His kisses became more demanding.

To Helsa it was an ecstasy she had never known.

A wonder beyond any words and beyond all reason and thought.

She had always imagined in her dreams that when a man she loved kissed her it would be wonderful.

But this was like flying to Heaven and dancing with the stars.

The Duke felt that it was the kiss of real love that had always eluded him and he had begun to believe that it only ever existed in novels.

He recognised as he kissed Helsa again and went on kissing her his feelings for her were completely different from anything he had experienced in his life before.

It was not just the fiery desire that would flare up so quickly and would then die as rapidly as it had risen.

It was a sensation so perfect and so exquisite that it could only have come from Heaven.

As the Duke kissed Helsa, the wonder she felt was almost too much to be borne.

She gave a little murmur and hid her face against his neck and he could feel the beating of her heart against his.

Her whole body trembled with the ecstasy she was feeling and which he felt too.

For a moment they were silent.

Then he breathed softly,

"I love you, my beautiful darling, and I believe that you love me."

"I love you," Helsa whispered, "but I did not know that love – could be so perfect and so overwhelming."

The Duke raised his head.

Very gently he put his fingers under Helsa's chin and turned her glorious face up to his.

"You are so incredibly lovely, my darling. At the same time so clever and so intelligent that I am finding it hard to believe you really exist."

"How could you love me – like this?" Helsa asked him. "When we hardly know each other?"

"I have been searching for you ever since I grew up and became a man and I could never understand why every woman I met, however beautiful and however charming eventually disappointed me. I know now it was because she was not *you*."

His voice was quiet and tender.

Helsa looked up into his eyes and she realised that every word he spoke was true and came from his heart.

"In all my dreams," she whispered, "I believed that one day I would find a man like you. But as I walked back here this afternoon and knew that I loved you – I thought I would never see you again."

"What we were talking about just now was that you should look after me and protect me from Lady Basset and all predators like her."

"You know I want to – " Helsa murmured.

"Then the sooner we are married, the better," the Duke sighed.

Helsa's eyes opened wide.

The Duke smiled at her and he knew exactly what she was thinking before she posed the question.

"I am asking you in a rather roundabout fashion to be my wife. My darling Helsa, I know that we will be the happiest couple there has ever been."

Because she could not find a single word to reply to him, Helsa would have hidden her face again.

But the Duke prevented her.

He found her lips with his and kissed her until they were both breathless.

Then they stood still, the Duke holding Helsa close in his arms.

Suddenly there was the sound of footsteps and the study door opened.

For a moment it was impossible for Helsa to come back from the enchanted world the Duke had taken her into.

Then with an effort she disentangled herself from his arms.

And as her father came into the room, she managed to splutter,

"I – was waiting for you – Papa."

"So I see," the Vicar smiled faintly.

Then he looked towards the Duke and exclaimed,

"You must be Victor. You have grown a lot since I last saw you, but you are very like your father."

Helsa had reached her father's side and was holding up her face to kiss him.

Now she stared in astonishment as he walked over to the Duke holding out his hand.

"I had no idea you were to be a guest at The Hall, Victor, and I am certain that you came here to win the steeplechase."

The Duke looked bewildered, took the Vicar's hand and then he cried,

"But, of course, you are my father's great friend, Alfred Irvin, but somehow I just never connected you with Irvin Hall!"

"That is not really surprising, as I cannot afford to live there, and it was not mine when your dear father was alive."

"*Yours*?" the Duke asked incredulously, "but Lady Basset told me it belonged to *her*."

The Vicar smiled.

"She was obviously trying to impress you, Victor, But she was only a tenant, whom I might say I was very grateful to have as there was no chance after the war of my ever being able to afford to take my father's place."

"I remember now my father talking about you," the Duke said, "and telling me you had come into the title."

"For what it is worth," the Vicar replied. "But, as everyone here knows me as 'the Vicar', it would only have complicated matters even more if I had taken up the title. So Helsa and I let things remain as they always had been."

The Duke was silent as if with surprise and then her father glanced at Helsa and remarked,

"I thought when I came into the study that you and my daughter must be well acquainted with each other!"

The Duke smiled.

"I was actually asking someone very beautiful, who has just saved me from an unbelievable nightmare to be my wife."

The Vicar stared at him.

"*Your wife!*" he repeated. "My dear boy, I cannot think of anyone I would rather have as a son-in-law than your father's son!"

"And I cannot imagine anyone," the Duke replied, "lovelier, more ethereally beautiful or more adorable than your glorious daughter."

He took Helsa's hand in his as he was speaking and realised that she was trembling.

At the same time her eyes were shining.

The Duke thought no one could look more radiant than she did.

With difficulty Helsa managed to say,

"I think we must now tell Papa – exactly what has happened. He will think it most strange that you did not know my surname when you came here just now."

The Vicar looked from one to the other in surprise.

"What *has* been happening?" he asked. "I thought that, as Helsa was staying at The Hall, you must have met each other there."

Helsa gave a little laugh.

"It's all so complicated, Papa. We must start at the beginning. Although you may be angry with me for doing so, I must tell you why I stayed to The Hall."

Her father was listening intently and she went on,

"It was not just to see that all was going well, but to act as lady's maid to Lady Basset."

"Lady's maid! Why on earth should you have to do that, Helsa?"

"Because Mary Emerson, who had promised to do so, had to go to the deathbed of her grandmother at the last moment."

"Oh, is the old lady dead? I am sorry about that, but she has been very poorly for years."

"Yes, I know, Papa, but as there was no one else we could trust to look after Lady Basset, I took her place."

"We met by chance," the Duke intervened. "The moment I saw Helsa I thought she was the most beautiful girl I have ever seen in my whole life."

The Vicar smiled.

"Exactly what I thought about her mother when *we* first met."

"Then I saw her riding," the Duke went on as if the Vicar had not spoken. "I thought that she must have come down from Heaven and was an angel on horseback. There are no other words to describe the way she looked."

"So you fell in love – ?"

There was a pause before Helsa suggested,

"I think that Papa should know – exactly what did happen. It will help us to decide what you can do about it."

The Vicar then looked quizzically from one to the other.

"What has been going on?" he demanded.

"You will find it hard to believe," said Helsa, "but every word of the story we are going to tell you is the truth and the whole truth."

"I should hope so," the Vicar added.

"I will tell you my part, Papa."

"Well, at least let us sit down while you do so, my dear."

The Vicar seated himself in one of the armchairs by the fireplace, as Helsa slipped her hand into the Duke's, drawing him down beside her on the sofa.

She told her father in as few words as possible how she had climbed up to the roof of the tower for a good view of the start of the steeplechase.

How Lady Basset and the man called Silas Tybolt had come into the room below and it was then that she had overheard the plot they had concocted, to kidnap the Duke when he reached the top of Monk Wood and take him into the slate mine.

There to be drugged by a drink he would take in ignorance to relieve the dryness of his throat because of the slate, and he would then be married to Lady Basset by a genuine Priest and their marriage would be witnessed by two men.

Helsa went on to relate how she had rushed down from the roof as soon as Lady Basset and her accomplice had left.

How she had taken the Duke's second stallion, the only one left in the stables.

How she had galloped as quickly as she could the shortest way to Monk Wood to warn him.

The Vicar had remained silent all the time she was talking and now he exclaimed,

"I have heard quite enough of such a disgraceful and tortuous plot. You were lucky that when Victor heard your story, he actually believed you."

"I found it difficult," agreed the Duke. "But I knew that no one as really lovely and so obviously good as your daughter would ever tell a lie."

He smiled at Helsa before he continued,

"So I did as she told me and rode back pretending my horse had sprained a leg. Then, collecting everything I had at The Hall, I came straight here to the Vicarage to wait for Helsa."

"I thought he had driven back to London," Helsa added. "But I found when I returned to The Hall that Mary had arrived to take over from me. So I came to find you, Papa, to tell you all that had happened."

"I really find it the most incredible story I have ever heard," said the Vicar, "and, of course, that woman had no right to pretend to be a relation of ours. At the same time I can understand, Victor, that you were impressed by Irvin Hall even though it is in a pretty poor condition."

"Is it really impossible for you to live there?" the Duke then asked.

The Vicar threw up his hands.

"It is difficult, my dear boy, for me to live here, let alone in a place of that size. The men my father employed on the estate went off to the Crimean War. As you know very few returned. Thus the land has been neglected and the house needs extensive repairs. So I could only keep on hoping against hope that things would improve."

"Because Papa could not afford the stipends of the Parsons he has been looking after three Parishes," Helsa came in, "and it is far too much for him."

For the first time since he had been sitting there, the Duke released her hand.

He bent forward and turned to the Vicar,

"I think, Uncle Alfred, as I always called you when I was a boy, that if you will forgive me for saying so, you are being very stupid."

The Vicar raised his eyebrows.

"In what way?"

"If you have a slate mine, which I understand was quite a large and profitable one in the past, it could now be a gold mine to you."

The Vicar stared at him.

"What do you mean?" he asked.

"You must realise if you have visited London lately that there has been a huge explosion of rebuilding and new construction. Slate, I happen to know personally, has risen enormously in price and is most difficult to obtain."

Helsa gave a cry of excitement.

"You mean we can sell our slate?"

"I have a small mine on my own estate which I am trying to develop," said the Duke. "Every ton that comes out of it is in demand from half-a-dozen builders. You will have more demand than I have as you are nearer London."

"I must say that it never struck me that anything I owned was saleable," the Vicar observed. "The pictures, furniture and everything else of any value at The Hall are naturally entailed."

The Duke smiled.

"Of course they are and you are very lucky it has all been reasonably well preserved. When I was taken round The Hall by Lady Basset I was, as it happens, exceedingly impressed by everything she told me her ancestors had left her!"

"Her ancestors are entirely part of her imagination," the Vicar replied. "Meanwhile the house, and I just cannot believe that one slate mine can really save it, will go on decaying as it was doing before it was hastily put in order, apparently to impress you, Victor!"

"I am glad to have been of service," the Duke said cynically. "But now I have an even better idea and I hope you will agree to it."

The Vicar looked at him questioningly.

"I am listening, Victor."

"I have been thinking for some time that I need a place for my racehorses near London. Mervinston Castle is too far North and I have been looking for a site near Newmarket. But this would be far more convenient."

The Vicar stared at him.

"What are you suggesting, Victor?"

"I am suggesting that you take over half the house as your own and let Helsa and me have the other half. I have a feeling that you will be asked to run the whole place when we are not with you."

He smiled at Helsa before he continued,

"We will enlarge the stables and then make a local Racecourse, which is definitely needed near London, out of the present paddock and the fields beyond it."

The Vicar was staring as if he could hardly believe what he was hearing.

"Are you seriously suggesting this?" he asked.

"On one condition – which is that you give me your daughter as my wife as quickly as possible. Quite frankly I cannot live without her and I need her to protect me from harridans like Lady Basset!"

"I promise I will, Victor," cried Helsa.

She looked up at the Duke and for a long moment neither of them could look away.

Watching them the Vicar was silent.

And then he said,

"I wonder if I am going to suggest something you will not like. In which case you must say so at once."

"What is that?" the Duke wanted to know.

"It is that, if you really love each other, as I believe you do, then you should be married immediately. Neither of you is going to be happy if you are so concerned about Lady Basset's intentions. She may wish to avenge herself, as the plan she spent so much money on has failed."

"I am sure that is absolutely true," responded the Duke. "What do you think, my darling?"

He turned to Helsa as he spoke and, as she looked up at him, there was no need for words.

They both knew how much they needed each other.

"Very well," he said, "the answer is 'yes'. My only other question is, 'when will you marry us?'"

"I was thinking that it could be either this evening or tomorrow morning, Victor."

Helsa drew in her breath.

"As quickly as that! Perhaps, Victor, you will want time to consider and to think again – "

The Duke laughed and interrupted her.

"Now you are talking nonsense, Helsa. You know what we feel for each other is something so wonderful, so fantastic and unbelievable that we must not play about with anything so perfect."

"Then what do you want?" Helsa asked him coyly.

"You! *Now*! At once. I will not feel safe until the ring is on your finger."

Again they were gazing into each other's eyes and the Vicar had been forgotten.

He rose to his feet.

"I will marry you," he announced, "this evening in my Church. You had better stay here tonight and leave for London tomorrow morning.

"It will be too late then for Lady Basset to conceive any more dastardly plots against you. She will not imagine for a moment that having set off for London you and your horses are actually here in my stables."

"Papa is entirely right," said Helsa. "Having been frustrated because you did not turn up at the top of Monk Wood, she may well have sent the Priest and the other two men to The Hall to look for you. Finding you are not there, they might go straight to London to find you."

"It sounds rather far-fetched. Equally I do think it would be a terrible mistake, Victor, for you to take any risks at this particular moment."

"I agree with you," the Duke replied, "and I will be very honoured if you will marry your daughter to me this evening."

"If I may suggest something else, for I think you should leave England immediately on your honeymoon. By the time you return Lady Basset will have doubtless vanished from the Social world and what has occurred here will be forgotten."

He looked thoughtful before he added,

"I will move into The Hall as soon as she leaves and try to make it as it used to be when my father and my grandfather were alive."

"That is all I ask and, of course, start work on the Racecourse."

"Now you are making one of the dreams of my life come true," sighed the Vicar. "It is something I have often thought about and a Racecourse at Irvin would be the most exciting venture I have ever planned or attempted to carry out."

"What is more, Papa, if we could make money from the slate mine, you will be able to afford to recruit other Priests for the three Parishes and you can retire. You have often said that is what you really want to do."

"That is true, my dear, I am really too old to run about from Parish to Parish and do what must be done for all those who need God's help."

He spoke simply and the Duke knew how much it meant to him and he then declared,

"Where I am concerned, I want you to understand that from now on money is no object. As soon as you can find them, you can pay the best Parsons available to take over the work you have done so brilliantly. What is more I want our Racecourse to be one of the best in the whole of the South of England!"

The two men smiled at each other and then Helsa exclaimed,

"If I am really to be married this evening, I have to find myself a dress to wear and also to tell Bessie we will be three for dinner. I am sure she will make us something very special."

"Now I know that as well as having a very lovely wife, I will have a very capable one," the Duke chuckled.

"She will look after you, Victor, as she has looked after me – with love and understanding and no woman can give you more.

"That reminds me, I must go and tell George when he has put away my horse not to go home. He will need to help your men find accommodation if they too are staying the night."

"There is plenty of room in the attic," said Helsa. "Also, Papa, it will be a bit of a squeeze in the stables, and you must tell George that your horse as well as Golden Arrow can be put out in the field."

"I will tell him, my dear, and he had better go and collect Victor's men."

"They are not far up the road," the Duke chipped in, "and I told one of my grooms to be loitering near your gates in an hour, which should be nearly up by now."

"I can see that you have thought of everything and that reminds me very much of your father, Victor. He had a head for detail which was better than anyone else's I have ever met."

The Vicar then left the room and closed the door.

The Duke had risen to his feet and now he put out his hand to draw Helsa to hers.

"I don't believe that this is real." she whispered. "It cannot be true – and I know I am going to wake up soon."

"If you do, it will be in my arms, and I will be able to assure you that everything I have promised will come true and a great deal more as well – "

"It is so wonderful that I feel you are an archangel come down from Heaven, Victor, to save us from the mess and misery we have been in and which we felt would only grow worse and worse every year."

"Now it is going to be better and better, my darling Helsa, and your father will, I know, enjoy every moment of creating a brand new Racecourse and most important of all making The Hall blossom again."

"How can you say such wonderful things to me," Helsa enthused, "and how can I have been so lucky as to have found you?"

The Duke smiled.

"I think as it happens, my precious, I found you. I thought when I saw you walking towards the stables, you were the most beautiful and exquisite creature I had ever dreamt about and that it was impossible for her to exist."

"Do you really think – we will be happy?"

The Duke put his arms around her and drew her close to him.

"I know when I hold you like this," he breathed, "that you are everything any man could want and a great deal more besides. But, my darling, I am going to answer your question in the only practical way – "

As he finished speaking his lips found hers.

Once again he was kissing her as he had before.

Kissing her until they were both once again swept into an ecstasy that was not of this world.

He kissed her and went on kissing her until they both recognised that they were not two people but one.

Their thoughts, their feelings and their love were a miracle which had come down from Heaven to unite them.

"I love you, my darling," the Duke murmured.

It was difficult for Helsa to speak, but she knew as she moved closer and ever closer to him that she had found perfection.

It was what every man and every woman seeks, but only a few are privileged to find.

It was a perfection in which two people think the same, are the same and are part of each other.

Theirs was a love that would not diminish with the years but increase.

It was a love so incredibly perfect and so much a part of Heaven itself that Helsa believed they would never lose each other in this life nor in the thousands of lives yet to come.

They would love, work and think together.

And in their own way bring as much happiness and comfort to others as well as to themselves.

There was so much for them to do and so much that needed doing.

Every moment they were together would be one of divine happiness.

"I love you, Victor," Helsa mumbled when at last she could speak.

Her voice seemed to come from a depth within her she had not fathomed before.

"I love and adore you, my angel," the Duke replied. "We have found each other and now nothing can hurt or destroy what we have together. How could I have been so lucky?"

"That is just what I was asking about you," Helsa smiled.

"It has been a steeplechase of our very own – "

"A steeplechase for love!"

"And we have both won!"

"We have both won, my darling Victor, and no one in the future can ever overcome us."

Helsa wanted to tell him that she would protect and look after him for the rest of their lives, but there was no need for words.

The Duke was kissing her wildly, passionately and fervently.

She felt they were already flying above the earth and touching the glory of the sun.

It was theirs and the world beyond the world was theirs too.

The World of Love where they were together and would remain together for the rest of time.

No man or woman could ask for more.

It was only as the Duke kissed her again that Helsa was able from the depths of her soul to pray,

'Thank You, God, thank You.'

She had saved him and he was hers.

Just as God had brought them both together, so He would look after them and protect them for all Eternity.